Legend of
Zandora
Birth of the Maiden
KAREN DEITERING WILSON
Illustrated by Sonny Heston

This publication contains the opinions and ideas of its author. It is intended to provide helpful and informative material on the subjects addressed in the publication. The author and publisher specifically disclaim all responsibility for any liability, loss or risk, personal or otherwise, which is incurred as a consequence, directly or indirectly, of the use and application of any of the contents of this book.

WORKBOOK PRESS LLC
187 E Warm Springs Rd,
Suite B285, Las Vegas, NV 89119, USA

Website: https://workbookpress.com/
Hotline: 1-888-818-4856
Email: admin@workbookpress.com

Ordering Information:
Quantity sales. Special discounts are available on quantity purchases by corporations, associations, and others.
For details, contact the publisher at the address above.

Library of Congress Control Number:
ISBN-13:   978-1-958176-76-4 (Paperback Version)
                978-1-958176-77-1 (Digital Version)

REV. DATE: 25/03/2022

Legend of ZANDORA

Legend of Zandora

Birth of the Maiden

Karen Deitering Wilson

To My Children Grandchildren

And

Beloved Brian

Many say; these are only foolish myths, dreamed up by the imagination of insanity, but I say; "Who is really the insane one? For insanity, if not all, does have some merit to it."

CONTENTS

INTRODUCTION

(In the Land of Zandora AD 600)

Haunted by Merlin's prediction, King Torin knew that not only was his kingdom at stake, but the different kingdoms of the world would also see his firstborn's wickedness grow. Peace and prosperity would never bless the land until a maiden born of mortal and Zandorian blood took up the challenge to fight this iniquity. Merlin made it clear that unless the tribes of the different worlds came together to help this maiden, the evil would destroy life as they knew it.

With caution, Merlin gave the secret of this maiden's identity to King Torin and three of King Torin's trusted kinsmen. Merlin said, "The mark of the red dewdrop crystal will appear on the maiden's forehead upon her birth. Whoever shall witness this birth shall keep her identity a secret, for if anything happens to this child, the only hope in bringing back the balance of life to the land of Zandora will be lost forever."

And so became the legend of Zandora.

CHAPTER 1
BIRTH OF A MAIDEN

(Present Day)

Pull over! Pull over!" Heather screamed. "I'm not going to make it to the hospital. This child is coming!" Draco pulled the car over to the side of the road. The only sign of life besides Draco, his wife, and his mother, Morwenna, were the trees hovering over the isolated dirt road. Morwenna helped her daughter-in-law out of the car while her son ran to the trunk and pulled out a blanket for his wife to lie on. Under the bright light of the moon, Morwenna noticed her son's pale face as he held Heather's hand. She knew she had to do something before he passed out.

"Draco, do you hear water splashing against rocks?" she asked. "I need you to go and get us some water. I believe the pail we used yesterday to collect shells is still in the back of the car; you can use that. Now go!"

Draco went to retrieve water while Morwenna helped Heather get ready to deliver her child. She held her hand as Heather moaned with another contraction.

"This little one is like its father," Morwenna said softly. "Did I ever tell you the story about how Draco's life began under the stars?"

Heather looked at Morwenna and tried to smile. "I guess we started a family tradition." Another contraction came, and she let out a yell.

Knowing they were out of time, Morwenna positioned herself to help Heather deliver the child. "Are you ready?"

"I don't think it's up to me," she said and took in a deep breath as the contractions continued.

Morwenna kept time and felt Heather's abdomen as the contractions came closer together. "Okay, I want you to push when I say push." As Morwenna gave the instruction, Heather gave out one long and loud scream, and then an eerie silence fell over them. Morwenna cradled the child in her arms.

"It's a girl!" she shouted, taking off her shawl to wrap the child.

Unable to hear her child, Heather became scared. "Why isn't she crying?"

It was as if Morwenna never heard Heather's question while she held the baby's limp body in her arms. "Come on, breathe, breathe," Morwenna whispered. Still not breathing, the child was too still as Morwenna held her upside down by the legs and smacked her backside. She then turned the child upright and blew lightly on the child's lifeless blue lips. "It's time you met the world."

The child suddenly jerked, gasping for her first breath, and then wiggled her tiny pink legs and arms. "She's strong." Morwenna laughed and placed the baby into Heather's arms.

The baby's tiny cries traveled through the branches of the trees to Draco's ears, and with pail in hand he instantly ran to be with his wife and child. Out of breath, he dropped to his knees to get closer to Heather. "It's a Girl." she whispered to Draco.

Can I hold her?" he asked, and Heather placed the child into his arms. He beamed at his daughter as he rocked her in his arms. "She's beautiful and so perfect. Just look at her tiny fingers and toes." Draco stood and turned to his mother as he noticed a mark forming on the baby's forehead. "Mother," he whispered, "do you see what I see?"

Morwenna nodded as the two of them watched a tiny red dewdrop form on the child's forehead under the light of the harvest moon, only to disappear soon after. Morwenna lifted the child from her son's arms.

"I shall call you Autumn Mist, but your full name will be Autumn Jorah Mist: Autumn after the colorful leaves that surrounded you tonight, Jorah after the rain, and Mist from the dewdrop that danced upon your forehead."

Heather looked at Draco then back at Morwenna. "Actually, Morwenna, Draco and I have already decided names. If it was a girl, we wanted to call her Paige."

Morwenna hesitated for a moment. "That may be so, but this child is no ordinary child. She is from the blood of two different worlds, and for that reason she shall bear the names of two different worlds."

Without another word, she looked at the moon overhead and then took the freezing river water Draco had collected. She placed her hand into the pail, and the water changed from icy cold to ninety-five degrees, the perfect temperature in which to bathe a child. Morwenna tore a small piece from the shawl that wrapped Autumn Mist and proceeded to wash her grandchild. Afterward, like a baptism, Morwenna held up the child and called to the heavens.

"Paige shall be your mortal name, given to you by your parents, but let it also be known that on this day the heavens have marked you. You shall be known to the world of the Zandorians as Autumn Jorah Mist, Maiden of Zandora."

CHAPTER 2
FRUSTRATED

(Seventeen Years Later)

Bang! The old screen door hammered against the wooden doorframe when Paige stormed out of the house. "I can't believe her," she rambled as she slammed shut the door of her Volkswagen Beetle. "If Mom thinks I'm going to wear that stupid swimsuit of hers, she can think again. It's bad enough wearing this old hand-me-down cheesecloth dress, but at least it's not as stupid as wearing her outdated swimsuit."

Her temper tantrum in full swing, she sped out of the driveway with a squeal of tires and raced away from the house. She never noticed the police car on the side of the road until lights flashed in her rearview mirror. *Oh great, a cop.*

Nervously, she glanced at her speedometer and then pulled her car over to the side of the road. She rolled down the window when the officer approached.

"Turn off your engine," he instructed. "I need to see your driver's license, registration, and proof of insurance."

Paige turned off the ignition and then fumbled through her purse before she remembered her registration and insurance card were in the glove compartment.

"Do you know how fast you were going, young lady? You were going sixty-two in a fifty-five."

Paige handed the officer the documents he requested and batted her eyes in hopes that he would let her off with a warning. "I'm sorry, but my mind was on an argument I had with my mom earlier."

The officer glanced at her as he took her papers, and then he went back to his cruiser. Paige tapped her fingers on the steering wheel while she wiggled her right foot up and down. She continued to gaze into the rearview mirror as the officer spoke on his car radio. A few minutes passed before the officer got out of his cruiser and returned to her.

"I'll tell you what I'm going to do. I'll let this one slide with a warning, but if I see you doing even one mile over the speed limit again, I'll write you up. Understand?" he asked before he handed back her information. "Next time you have an argument with your mother, I recommend you don't get behind the wheel."

"Yes, sir." Paige took her papers and put them away before she started up the car. That was close. I can only imagine what Mom would have said if I got a ticket, she thought as she slowly made her way back onto Highway 41.

It wasn't long before Paige found herself turning onto an old, unmarked dirt road that led to a line of trees. Like a child chasing after an ice cream truck, she shivered with excitement, for just beyond the line of trees was a beach with an endless view of the lake.

The breeze from the water's edge rolled into the car through the open window. The aroma of fish filtering to Paige's nose brought back images of her father driving the same road. Even though he had disappeared several years before, his voice continually haunted her daily life. "Breathe in that air. Can you smell the fish?" her father's voice echoed in her head.

While the car rocked and bounced over potholes and washout ruts, she spoke as if her father were sitting next to her. "Yes, Dad. You'd have to be dead not to smell it."

She parked the car several feet from the beach. For several minutes she sat motionless, her arms wrapped around the steering wheel, and stared out the windshield. A man and child collected shells from the beach, and it brought flashbacks of her and her father doing the same thing many years ago.

Paige got out of her car as the two disappeared down the shoreline. She closed her eyes and tilted her face toward the sun, allowing its rays to beam heat onto her face. She inhaled the fresh air and welcomed the hot white sand that blanketed her feet. After getting the kinks out of her body, she retrieved a wide-brim hat and a wicker basket from the front seat, then slipped off her sandals and tossed them inside her car. With her hat on and her basket securely in hand, she headed to the water's edge, barefoot and free, and whispered, "Maybe today I'll be lucky, Dad, and a wave will wash up the agate I need to bring you home."

CHAPTER 3

FIRST ENCOUNTER

A chill ran down her spine as the hot, dry sand under her feet turned wet and cold. She felt some relief from the sun as the breeze blew through her dress, filling it like a balloon around her lean body, and whisked her long, curly hair away from her sweaty neck. Paige's mother never allowed her to wear makeup because she believed her unblemished olive complexion, dark green eyes, and ruby red lips had more perfection than those of any goddess or princess.

While Paige was occupied gathering shells and other trinkets off the beach, three young men were busy building elaborate sand castles. All were tan and muscular, but Noah was taller than his friends were; in fact he towered over them. His shoulder-length blond hair shone in the sun the way a crystal reflects light, and his laughter echoed above the other two. It wasn't until Noah turned to work on the other side of the sand castle that he caught sight of a girl. He watched her for several minutes before he pointed over in her direction.

"You see that girl over there? Do you know who she is?"

"Never seen her before," Jake replied, while Sam just shook his head.

Noah smiled and continued to watch the girl. "She sure stands out from the scenery."

Jake smirked as he looked over at the girl. "If you ask me, she seems pretty weird. Look at that outfit."

"Forget the outfit; look at her," Noah protested.

Amused by the whole thing, Sam laughed. "Okay, Romeo, why don't you just go over and talk to her?"

Noah shrugged. "Maybe later; she looks busy."

"She doesn't look too busy to me. Besides, that's never stopped you from going over to meet a girl before."

Jake chuckled and tossed some sand at Noah. "Maybe he's scared."

"I'm not scared." Noah clenched his teeth and stood up to wipe off the sand.

Paige stopped collecting shells to watch seagulls and listen to their shrill kittee-wa-aaake, kittee-wa-aaa. Unlike most people, she discovered at a very young age that she could communicate with other creatures. She quickly learned not to tell anyone about her strange ability to speak to animals. The other children at school had been cruel to her, mocking her and calling her a liar. At least she found comfort knowing that her grandmother believed her.

A wave washed over her feet, and with it a shell washed onto the beach and caught her attention. As she bent down to pick it up, she spotted a boy unknown to her. *Oh great, someone is coming in this direction, covered in sand, no less. I don't need this right now.*

The boy smiled and stretched out his sandy hand to Paige. "Hi, I'm Noah. And you are?"

She said nothing as she fumbled with the basket lid. She watched as Noah's face flushed with frustration when she didn't respond. *Maybe he will go away if I ignore him.* She knew his pride was at stake when he withdrew his unshaken hand and continued with his questions.

"So, do you come here often?"

When she didn't reply, Noah bent down and placed his hand on her basket.

"Why don't you answer? Are you deaf?" He raised his voice, annunciating each word.

Paige looked away from the basket and glared at him. "Are you always this rude? Couldn't you see that I'm busy? And what business is it of yours if I come here often or not?" she snapped back.

Surprised by her attitude, Noah put his hands on his waist. "Sorry if I bothered you, but I was trying to make conversation. You sure are hotheaded for someone so…oh never mind." He turned to walk away, waving his arms in frustration.

"Funny, one could say the same thing about you!" she yelled after him.

He did a turnabout and faced her. "At least I'm not the rude one. I just asked if you come to the beach often. What's the big deal?"

Silence filled the air as he stepped closer to Paige. She wrapped her arms around her basket and took a few steps backward. Noah, still frustrated, broke the silence.

"I noticed that you were picking things up off the beach and thought maybe we had something in common. Why are you so defensive anyway?"

"Defensive? Why shouldn't I be? You came over here and bothered me. Now excuse me, but I have to go." She tried to mimic Noah when he turned away from her, but instead she lost her footing. "Ooooh!" she squealed as she started to fall.

Noah grabbed her with both hands like a quarterback catching a football. Never letting go, he went down with her. Paige's hat and basket flew into the air, and she hit the ground, landing on top of him.

"Are you okay?" he asked.

Paige felt as if her cheeks were on fire. She jumped to her feet and straightened her dress before she retrieved her hat and basket. Embarrassed, she looked everywhere but at Noah as she answered him. "I'm fine. Now if you don't mind, I have to go." She started away from him.

"Can you at least tell me your name so I know who I saved?"

She stopped and turned toward him. "You didn't save me, and my name is Paige!"

"What? I couldn't hear you."

"And you ask if I'm deaf?" she snapped. "I said my name is Paige."

"Paige. Nice name. Mine's Noah."

"You already told me your name." She rolled her eyes and stomped away, but she couldn't control the smile that stretched across her face. She was glad he couldn't see it, or hear her thoughts. Wow, what abs. And his eyes—how could anyone not notice his beautiful blue eyes?

Noah stood where he had fallen and watched Paige drift farther away. It wasn't until she was out of calling distance that he went back to the sand castle he had been building.

Jake couldn't wait to hear his explanation. "Well?" he asked. "I watched you put the moves on that girl. Did you?"

Before he could finish, Noah gave him a stern look. "She tripped and I caught her, that's all."

Jake grabbed his right arm. "Okay, if that's what you want us to believe, but we saw that girl on top of you. By the way, great move."

Noah's face became hot like burning charcoals. "She tripped, Jake!"

Seeing Noah step back to take a swing, Sam interrupted him. "It's okay, Noah. Jake doesn't know when to stop with the questioning. He'll harass you until you tell him what he wants to hear."

Noah looked at Sam, then at Jake, and then he shrugged and started to laugh. "It must have looked pretty funny— the two of us falling to the ground."

"Hey, Noah," Sam said, laughing along, "maybe you can give us lessons on how to do that fancy move. You know, in case we have to help a girl when she trips."

"Do you really think I'm going to share my secrets with the likes of you?" Noah teased as he went back to work on his sand castle.

"See, Sam? I told you Noah was trying to make a move on that girl. You owe me a lunch."

While Noah worked on the sand castle, Paige's thoughts drifted between Noah and the black agate. *Too bad I have a black agate to find. It may have been fun to share my day with Noah.*

She bent down and picked up a small rock, then held it to the sky so the sun could shine on it. "I should have been nicer," she mumbled. "If I had any brains, I could have told him I was collecting agates. He didn't have to know why I'm looking for a black agate. He would think I'm crazy."

She trembled at the thought of her grandmother's words: *An evil sorcerer holds your father captive.* She tossed the stone into the water. "I have to stay focused. Without that agate, I'll never see my father again. It has to be on this beach. River Otter told me so."

CHAPTER 4

SEARCHING FOR THE BLACK AGATE

The tide rolled in as the sun started to set. The only signs that anyone had been on the beach were Paige and the sand castle Noah had made earlier, and even that was being washed away by the tide.

"Paige!"

She jumped and turned to see who had shouted her name. "Noah! What do you think you're doing scaring me like that?"

"I didn't mean to scare you, but I wanted you to wait up."

"Wait up for what?" she demanded. "It's obvious that your friends left. Did you scare them away, too?"

"No, I wanted to apologize for the way I acted earlier. Besides, I brought you my jacket. If you hadn't noticed, the sun is going down. I thought you might be cold in that dress."

Paige smiled as she allowed him to put his jacket around her shoulders. "I was pretty mean to you, too. Apology accepted."

"I see you're still collecting things off the beach. Find anything interesting to add to your basket?" he asked, trying to look inside.

She brought her basket closer to her chest. "Why are you so interested?"

"There you go again, being defensive," Noah snapped back. "If you don't want me to know, just say so."

Paige stared into his eyes while he continued to speak. "And what are you staring at?"

"Your eyes; I've never seen eyes so blue. They're bluer than the bluest sky I've ever seen."

Noah's face turned apple red, and he coughed into his hand. "So, why are you still out here?" he asked to change the subject.

Paige hesitated. "I'm searching for items that could be used to make jewelry. See this?" She held up the necklace around her neck so that he could get a closer look at it. "My dad made this for me. It's from an agate I found. It is everything to me."

Noah examined the necklace. "I've collected a lot of interesting things that have washed up on the shore too: old coins, shells, and things that I don't even know what to call."

She stepped a little closer to him. "I doubt you have what I'm looking for."

"Maybe, but I must tell you, I've collected things from many different beaches for many years."

"Well then, do you have a black agate?" She smiled as she leaned against his arm. "My dad told me that if you could find a black agate, it was like finding the pot of gold at the end of the rainbow."

"A black agate. Hmm…" Noah tossed a couple of stones into the water before turning back to her. "I've never seen an agate in that color. Maybe the black agate you're looking for is like that pot of gold. You hear about it, but no one has actually seen it."

Disappointed, Paige glanced down at her feet and tapped on her basket before she looked back at him. "Maybe you're right, Noah, but people still search for that pot of gold."

"I'm sorry, Paige. I didn't mean it the way it came out. It's fine to believe in something magical. Without our dreams and imagination, life would be boring. I was just trying to say…oh never mind." Noah picked up a couple more stones and tossed them into the water.

They both fell silent as they strolled down the beach, separated only by the wind that blew between them. The only sound was that of the waves splashing onto the shoreline. "Wait! I just thought of something," Noah said, his voice ringing out. "I might have what you're looking for after all. I picked up this stone the other day; it may be your black agate. It's really unusual. If you want, we can go over to my house. I'll even let you look over my whole collection. I live about an hour from here; how about it?"

"And this is line number what," she laughed, "to convince a girl to go home with you?"

"I'm not making it up, Paige. I really found this unusual stone. It's like no other. I was going to toss it back into the water, but when I looked at it more closely, I noticed the unique lacing in it as I held it up to the light, I decided to keep it."

Paige had not found the black agate, and she didn't want to leave anything to chance. "I'll tell you what—give me your phone number, and I'll call to make arrangements to come over."

"You'll call me? I've heard that before."

"Noah, if I said I would call, I'll call—unless that's a problem."

For a moment, he said nothing. "Okay, Paige, my uncle's business card is in the left pocket of my jacket. It has the phone number where you can reach me."

She lifted an eyebrow. "You live with your uncle?"

"Since I was two. It's a long story. Maybe I'll tell you about it someday."

She took the card out of his jacket and read it. "You live on Rune Ridge. Never heard of it."

"It's the next county over." He chuckled. "I'll give you directions when you call; that way you'll have something to write on. I wouldn't want you to get lost."

"Don't worry, Noah. Believe it or not, girls can find their way around." She looked down at her watch. "I have to go; I'm late for dinner. My mom insisted that we have dinner together tonight. I promise I'll call you tonight; then we can make plans where to meet." She took off his jacket and handed it to him.

Noah held onto her hand. "Before you go, can I have your phone number—or can I drive you home?"

She withdrew her hand from his grip. "I'll give you my number when I call you. And thanks, but I have my own car. I'll be fine," she assured him as she walked away. She didn't look back until she felt that she was far enough away from him. "I'll call you tonight," she yelled, but when she turned to wave good-bye, Noah was already gone.

CHAPTER 5

RIVER OTTER'S CONCERNS

Excited to get back to her car, Paige followed a river that drained into Lake Superior. She couldn't get her mind off Noah. *He has to have the black agate.*

"Careful!" Otter screamed when Paige almost stepped on him.

"Oh! Sorry, Otter; I didn't see you there."

"Obviously. Why are you in such a hurry?"

"The black agate. I think I know where it is."

Otter looked surprised. "You do?"

"Yes, I do. I searched everywhere for that agate and found nothing, but I think Noah has it."

"Noah? Who's Noah?" asked Otter. "And how do you know he has the black agate?"

Paige was so eager to share her news with Otter that she could hardly get her words out. "It's a long story, but in short, I met this guy on the beach. At first I was very rude because I didn't want him to know what I was up to. Well, we both were ill mannered. Anyway, when we met up again, we started to talk."

"What did you talk about that makes you think he has the agate?" Otter asked.

"I found out Noah likes to collect things off the beach. I couldn't just ask him if he had a black agate, so I made up this story about my father telling me if I ever found a black agate, it was like finding a pot of gold at the end of the rainbow. Pretty clever story, if I do say so myself. Anyway, Noah said he likes to collect things off the beach—oh, I already said that—"

Otter held up his paws. "Slow down, Paige, you're talking too fast, and please stop pacing. You're making me dizzy."

She bent down to talk to him. "You don't understand. Noah mentioned that he had this stone that was so different. I've looked everywhere on that beach and haven't found the black agate. He has to have it."

"And if he does, what then?"

"I'll use my charm and wit, and hopefully Noah will give it to me. I wasn't very polite when we first met, but when I looked into his blue eyes, something told me I could trust him. It was the strangest thing."

Otter hesitated. "So, you should know soon if he has the black agate or not."

"I told Noah I'd call him tonight. If he does have the agate, my plan is to have it in my hands no later than tomorrow night."

"This concerns me, Paige. Could you do me a favor?" he asked. "Don't do anything until I check something out. You're in dangerous territory right now. I know you haven't spoken to your grandmother since your father disappeared, but I really think it's time you do."

"Have you forgotten? I can't call Grandma. Mom blames her for Father's disappearance. She screamed out some hateful words when Grandma tried to explain about the evil spell Father was under."

"Well then, you'll have to find another way to get in touch with her. Something is not right. You can't trust anyone—even Noah." Otter dove into the river. A few seconds later, he popped his head out and shouted, "Contact your grandmother." Then he vanished under the water.

CHAPTER 6
COMING OF AGE

(A Different Perception)

As Paige drove home from the beach that evening, she thought about how irritated her mother would be that she did not come home on time. She imagined her mother in the dining room, glancing at the old white plastic clock and wondering why she wasn't home, or how she might be on the front porch pacing and considering potential punishments. Suddenly, Paige couldn't stop the images of how worried her mother had been when her father had not returned home several years ago. She would never forget her mother's wide, glassy eyes when she glanced down at her watch, muttering, "Where is he?"

Unexpectedly, Paige felt emptiness in the pit of her stomach at the flashback of her mother's worries. How frantic she must be that she had not returned home. "I'd better hurry," she said and put her foot down on the gas.

Like most teenagers, Paige found herself isolated in that bewildering transition from childhood to maturity, a period when everything goes awry. All the negativity Heather had tried to conceal from her to protect her childhood innocence was now distorted by her constant exposure to the media's stories of violence and sex.

Adding to Paige's confusion were the changes occurring to her body, which sometimes brought self-consciousness and insecurity. She found herself trapped in a life that envied adulthood. The desire to grow up too fast caused frustration with her mother who wished she could regress back to the idyllic simplicity of childhood.

Now deemed older and mature enough to handle the truths of adulthood, Paige found that the unconditional love and guidance she had received from Heather had changed. She no longer felt that she could freely speak her mind, and her mistakes weren't so easily forgiven.

Her innocent and naïve fits of anger, worry, and guilt were replaced by resentment, apprehension, contempt, and lack of respect for her mother's discipline. Paige had witnessed how the years marched on relentlessly for Heather, and she felt that something inside of her had died when her father disappeared.

Heather's passion for living had declined; the latest fashions she used to enjoy wearing had turned into old, faded jeans, outdated sweatshirts, and a sentimental flowered sundress her father had bought her the day they purchased the home they lived in. She hardly laughed, had stopped wearing makeup, and pulled her flowing red hair back into a drab ponytail.

To Paige, she had gone from being the coolest mother to an irritating person who hadn't kept up with the times and who didn't take the time to understand her. She had a mother who had denied her the right to visit her grandmother, whom she loved dearly.

Paige's disappointment became overwhelming when she felt that her mother had been dishonest or indirect about her father's disappearance. She felt that if her mother had been honest from the beginning about her own faults, failures, and uncertainties, Paige could have carried herself through each day with empathy, understanding, and truth. But instead, Paige found comfort in knowing that her mother's frustration over her actions was to no avail. Paige knew her defiance was hurtful and wrong, but she didn't know how to stop being rebellious, so the vicious cycle of their fighting continued.

When Paige pulled up to the house, Heather was standing on the front porch with her arms folded, teeth clenched, foot tapping a continuous one-two-three, one-two-three rhythm. Without saying a word, Paige got out of her car and watched her mother's face turn dark red. Even before she could reach the steps, Heather's voice went into the low pitch she always used when she was angry.

"Where have you been, young lady? I was ready to call the police!"

Unwilling to go onto the porch, Paige stood at the base of the steps. "Mom, you knew I was going to the beach. I even asked you to come."

"You're almost two hours late, and I was worried."

Paige stayed where she was. "I'm sorry I'm late, Mom, but—"

"Sorry isn't going to cut it this time," she yelled as she turned to go inside the house.

Paige followed her into the house and tossed her hat on the table next to the door. "I said I was sorry. What more do you want?"

"Paige, don't talk to me in that tone! I was worried. You knew dinner was for six, and it's almost eight. I made it very clear that I wanted you home early so we could have dinner together. You could have called and told me you were going to be late."

Paige couldn't get a word in as Heather continued to scold her. "Raising you by myself hasn't been easy. Not calling and letting me know that you're okay is unacceptable."

Paige held up her cell phone, "I would have called, but my cell phone battery lost its charge."

Heather gave her a stern look, then waved her arms in frustration. It took a moment before she could collect her thoughts. "Maybe I should call my boss and tell him I can't leave. I don't know how I ever let him talk me into that promotion. But I can't go off to Ireland and leave you with Mrs. Palmer when you're like this. I'm not sure what it will take, or what I can do, to get through to you. I'm so tired of your attitude."

"I don't know. Maybe you could be a little more understanding or forgiving?"

"You know Paige, the more I let you do, the more you take, and the worse you get."

"Mom, I'm almost an adult, and believe it or not, I can make some decisions on my own."

"Don't get mouthy with me, Paige. Just because you're seventeen—"

"Almost eighteen."

"Just because you're seventeen doesn't give you the right to be thoughtless or disrespectful."

Silence filled the house as Paige followed Heather into the kitchen. "Tell you what, Mom." Paige paused for a second. "I promise I'll try to be more respectful, but you have to promise to be less angry."

"I'll tell you what. When you become more respectful, I promise to be less angry. I'm the parent, not you. I'll do the negotiations if there are negotiations to be done. All I ever asked is for you to be respectful."

Heather went to the fridge, took out the dinner she had cooked earlier, and placed it back into the oven. "Before I leave in the morning, do you think we can salvage what time we have together by not arguing? I'm tired, and I have too much on my mind to fight with you anymore."

"Fine." Paige's tone softened. "Just so you know; I'm really sorry for scaring you, Mom."

"I know, Paige. You're always sorry. Why don't you go upstairs and change while I put dinner back on the table?"

Paige went upstairs, and she stayed in her room until her mother called her down to eat. Like most dinners, they ate in silence. Afterward, Paige offered to clean up so Heather could finish her packing. Once the dishes were done, she went back upstairs and sat on her mother's bed.

"Mom, I need to ask you something, but I don't want to start another argument."

"I never said you couldn't ask me something, Paige. Nothing could ever be so bad that you can't ask."

"Okay. When I was at the beach today, I thought about Dad—"

"When don't you think about your father?"

"Just hear me out. When I was on the beach, I was missing Dad and Grandma. I know Dad left suddenly, and you blamed Grandma for Dad's disappearance, but it wasn't her fault."

"You're right; I do blame your grandmother. If it hadn't been for her making up stories, your dad would still be here, instead of going off—"

"Stop it, Mom! It's not Grandma's fault. Yes, Grandma had stories, but she told me the same stories, and I'm still here."

Heather stopped packing and sat next to her on the bed. "Okay, Paige, what's this really about?"

"I miss Grandma, Mom. I miss how we all used to sit on her porch and listen to the rain when it hit the tin roof. But what I miss the most about Grandma is the laughter." Paige grabbed her mother's hand. "Remember how we used to sit on her padded wooden swing—you know, the one bolted to the roof's rafters? Just the two of us. We would rock back and forth on that swing while Grandma found comfort in her old press back rocker."

Heather laughed as she gazed over at a photo hanging on the wall. It was a photo of Paige and her grandmother sitting on her front porch. "I remember. I used to say Morwenna was as hard-headed as that old rocker you see in that picture."

Paige went over to the photo Heather pointed at, took it off the wall, and then went back to sit beside her. "I remember Grandma's stories about a time when children actually played outside from sunrise to sunset, and how the children slept outside with only the moon and stars to cover them. I can't imagine living in a time with no TV, computers, or video games…having to always make up your own games to be entertained. I wonder if it became boring after a while to rely on playing instruments, singing songs, or reading books for entertainment?"

"I don't know, Paige. I recall you had a pretty good imagination yourself. Remember how you used to think you could talk to the animals when you were over at Morwenna's? Did you find it boring doing those things?"

"No, but I didn't live in a time when adventure was up to a kid's imagination. You know, when I look back on the times I spent with Grandma, I realize that she wanted to pass down her stories because it was important to her that we knew what her generation did and had. Grandma's stories brought life back to the dreamer who dared to have an imagination."

"Stop right there, Paige. I know where this is going. How you remember your grandmother and her stories is fine; I even looked the other way when she told stories of how she was the queen of Zandora and she ruled over other tribes and different worlds. The problem came when Morwenna tried to push her lifestyle onto us. I couldn't believe it when she told your father the day you were born that your destiny would be that of no mortal, and she named you Autumn Mist. Think about it, Paige—Autumn Mist."

"Mom, I don't care if Grandma had a pet name for me, so why should you?"

"It wasn't just the pet name she picked out for you. She wanted you to have an arranged marriage. She believed this marriage would bring the people of her world and ours together and, in doing so, would bring back harmony and stability to the land in which we live. I knew then there would be trouble. You have to understand, Paige, that your father and I wanted you to grow up with Morwenna's stories and imagination, but I made it very clear to your father that if he couldn't see that these were only stories, he would have to stop going over there. I know this seemed harsh but I had to put an end to your father's craziness. As Morwenna continued with her stories, your father became obsessed with them. He took off because he thought he had to save his family from some evil force."

"Mom, if you want to know the truth, my life became a mess when Dad disappeared, too. Not only did I lose a dad, but I also lost a grandmother. You blamed Grandma for Dad's disappearance. You didn't want to hear her explanation for why he vanished, and because of this, you've forbidden me to have any contact with her. You never asked me what I wanted."

Heather looked at her, and when she spoke, her voice quivered. "Paige, your grandmother repeatedly told that ridiculous story about the evil sorcerer Vindamar. She never stopped until your father believed he was the only one who could save you and the world from Vindamar and who knows what else. He thought it was his destiny to find some black agate so you didn't have to. I could understand you not knowing the difference between reality and fairy tales, but your father?"

"Are you done, Mom? I'm trying to tell you something, and all you do is blame, blame, blame. Will you listen for once?"

Heather took a long breath as she looked away from Paige. "I don't know if I can go through this again, Paige."

"Go through what? I know the difference between fairy tales and reality, so why do you keep me away from Grandma? All I'm asking is to talk to her. She's getting old; she won't be around much longer."

"Don't you think I haven't felt guilty about not letting you see your grandmother? I know she won't be here for long." Heather turned to walk away then stopped. "You're right. Maybe it's time you contacted her."

Paige jumped up and hugged her mother. "Honest? You're going to let me call her? You don't know how happy this makes me. Thanks, Mom. I'll call her right now."

"You want to call her right now?" Heather asked as she got up.

"Yes!" Paige exclaimed, following her downstairs to the living room.

Heather retrieved a piece of paper tucked away in an old address book. She hesitated before she held out the paper to Paige. "Here you go. I'm not sure if that number still works, or if she's even still alive. I'll be upstairs if you need me."

Paige's hand trembled as she took the tiny piece of paper from her mother's hand and went over to the phone. She couldn't believe that she was finally able to call her grandmother after so many years.

CHAPTER 7

A CALL TO GRANDMA MORWENNA

Paige's hands continued to shake as she dialed. She listened as the phone rang several times without any response. Just when she was ready to hang up, she heard a shaky, "Hello?"

"Grandma? It's me, Paige."

"Hello, dear. It's so good to hear from you. Otter told me that he asked you to call. He said you have been busy searching for a certain trinket to help your father."

"Yes, I have, and—"

"Autumn Mist, I hate to interrupt you, but why don't we talk about that when you come over tomorrow?"

"What do you mean, come over tomorrow?"

"You're telling me you haven't asked your mother about coming over yet? What's keeping you, Autumn Mist?"

"I don't know, Grandma. Maybe I should wait. Mom may tell me to hang up, and I won't be able to talk to you at all."

"You never know, my dear, unless you ask. Just come right out and ask her if you can come over while she is working overseas. I'll ask your mother if you like."

"No, Grandma, I'll ask." Paige put her hand over the phone and called out to her mother. "Mom, I have a huge favor to ask. Can I visit Grandma while you're in Ireland? Please, Mom?"

"I don't think so, Paige," she called back. "You know I've made plans for Mrs. Palmer to stay with you here. Besides, I doubt I could get an airline ticket so late."

"If I can get a ticket, can I go?"

Heather came into the living room and stood there for a brief moment before she took the phone from Paige. "Hello, Morwenna."

Paige watched as her mother listened to Morwenna and hoped for a sign that she would let her go. Finally Heather said, "Paige can go over if she can get a ticket. But," she emphasized the word, "you must promise me that you won't fill her head with nonsense. I don't want her going off to who knows where. And if Paige manages to get a ticket, she can only stay until I come back from overseas. Agreed?" She listened to Morwenna's response and then nodded. "Fine. Here's Paige." She handed the phone back to Paige and then went to the kitchen.

"Well, Grandma? What did you say?"

"I agreed to your mother's terms. Don't worry about getting a ticket; there is one waiting for you at the airport. All you need to do is call the airport and confirm you are going. It will be on the same plane as hers, so you can travel together. I guess I will see you tomorrow."

"I don't know how you do it, but you're amazing, Grandma. I'll see you soon."

Paige called the airport and confirmed her flight then ran to the kitchen. "Mom, you won't believe this—we're on the same flight. We don't part ways until you catch your international flight in Chicago. I'm going to Grandma's!" she shouted as she danced around the kitchen. "Mom, you don't know what this means to me. With summer almost over and you going to Ireland, I would have felt so alone."

"I'm happy for you, Paige, but I have to tell you I'm concern. I don't know what Morwenna said to make your father believe in all that nonsense, but don't allow her to do the same to you."

"Mom, you did a good job. Believe me, I'll be fine."

As her mother went upstairs, Paige went back to the living room. She had one more call to make. "Hello Noah!"

CHAPTER 8

NOAH

After leaving Paige at the beach, Noah went home to his uncle. Even though it was still summer, he felt an icy wind race down his back as he stood motionless in front of the huge house. He thought about how it looked as cold and empty as his uncle's eyes. He couldn't understand why his uncle would allow such an elaborate home to become so dirty and overgrown with weeds. The beautiful, tiny, French- style windows that once let in the sun's light were covered in years of built-up grime. The imported clay-tiled roof was blanketed in a mixture of centuries of dirt and weeds that concealed and harbored worms and other crawling creatures.

Noah looked at the cobblestone driveway that led up to the mansion's massive mahogany doors, admiring the way it circled around from his uncle's home of darkness. To Noah, that driveway was the only thing that had kept its natural beauty.

He didn't want to go in; he knew his Uncle Vindamar waited only for the answers he could get about Paige. He waited a few more seconds to build up his courage, and then he entered the house. He didn't even have a chance to hang up his jacket before his uncle's gigantic frame foreshadowed his arrival as he came down the grand staircase and into the foyer to question him.

"So tell me, what is this girl like?" Vindamar asked in his low, sinister voice.

"Defensive for the most part, but she seemed nice." He cleared his throat; his voice had squeaked, betraying his nervousness.

Perturbed, Vindamar stepped closer. "Did she tell you her last name, or why she was on the beach?"

"I told you, Uncle, she was defensive; she didn't talk much."

Vindamar glared at him. "I didn't send you back there to tell me she didn't talk much. I know she had something to say, and I want to know what it was."

Uncomfortable, Noah gave in. "Fine. Her name is Paige, and she was looking for trinkets. She said she likes to collect agates."

"Agates! What kind of agates?" he growled and stepped even closer.

"She wanted to find a black agate."

Vindamar grabbed Noah, digging his fingers into his shoulders. "What did you tell her?"

"I told her I had hundreds of them, but I didn't know if I had a black one or not."

"Good. Anything else?" he asked, easing the pressure on Noah's shoulder.

Noah managed to pull away from his grip. "I wanted to bring her here, but she had to go home. No offence, but I'm glad she couldn't make it. She may have thought I'm nuts living in a house like this. Besides she said she would call me. Now I know you've made it very clear I'm not to use any powers, but I had to use them to conjure up a business card. Before you say anything, it was just a business card—nothing more."

"You didn't put our real name on it, did you?" Vindamar roared like thunder, and Noah flinched.

"No, Uncle. Give me more credit than that. Your name is John Pain—you know you can be a pain sometimes." He started to laugh, which did nothing to lighten Vindamar's mood.

"This is no time to be funny, Noah. When are you going to see Paige again?"

"She's going to call me tonight."

Vindamar walked away from him and began to pace the foyer; he appeared to be thinking, or planning. "When Paige calls you, I want you to tell her that you were looking through your collection and that you believe you have what she is looking for."

"But I don't have the black agate. You do. Why would Paige need it anyway? She's a mortal."

"I'm not sure why she's looking for the black agate. That's why you're going to keep an eye on her for me. When she calls, I want you to make her believe you would do anything to help her look for whatever she needs. Got it?" he demanded.

"Okay, but she's not stupid. If she thinks I can't be trusted, she'll leave."

He tried to walk away, but Vindamar grabbed his arm. "Don't walk away from me. I'm not finished with you." He took a small rock out of his pants right pocket.

"I want you to give her this stone."

"Your black agate?"

"No, it's not the black agate, but she'll think it is." He laughed, placing the stone in Noah's hand just as the phone rang.

Noah pushed his way toward the other end of the foyer. "I have to get the phone. It might be Paige."

"Remember, Noah—I'm counting on you."

Noah tried to turn his back on Vindamar before answering the phone. "Hello?"

"Hi, Noah; it's me, Paige, from the beach. You said I could look at your collection. Would it be possible for you to bring it to my house tonight?"

"Tonight?" Noah's voice quivered.

"Sure, if it's not late. I'm curious about that rock you said was so unusual."

"Why don't you just come over tomorrow, Paige? We'll have more time to look at my collection. It's too big to carry around."

"I'm sorry. I guess you're right. It's just…well, I don't know you well enough to go to your house. You understand, don't you?"

"I guess so."

"Besides, I'm leaving to visit my grandmother tomorrow. I'll be there for a few weeks, and I wanted my mom to meet you before I left."

"Tell you what—since you seemed interested in my special rock, I'll bring that over. Will that work?"

"That's a great idea. How long will it take for you to get here?"

"I'm not sure. You never gave me your address."

"That's right; how stupid of me. Do you know where the Lake Fanny Hooe Resort and Campground is?"

"Sure."

"Well, I live near the campground. Just go to the third gravel road off Manganese. There are only two homes: an old abandoned house everyone says is haunted, and ours."

"You live in that big log house on the left?" he asked. "My uncle told me a story or two about that old house next to yours. I was about four when he took me there one night, but I was too afraid to keep my eyes open. It will take me an hour or so to get there."

"Great. See you soon, Noah."

Vindamar snickered as Noah hung up the phone. "So, you will be going to Paige's house tonight. Remember to give her that stone. I'll be here waiting to see how things went. Now go; you must not keep her waiting."

CHAPTER 9

THE GIFT

W hat are you doing?" Heather asked as Paige started to tidy up the living room.

"I've invited a boy over. His name's Noah, and I met him at the beach today."

"Why is he coming over? I thought you needed to get ready to go to your grandmother's."

"He's bringing something over for me to look at; he won't be here long. Mom, can you do me a favor and get the door when he shows up? I need to go upstairs and pack, and I don't want him waiting outside."

"I would love to meet this person," she replied with an arched eyebrow.

It wasn't long before Noah knocked on the door, and Heather answered as promised. She smiled and motioned Noah to come in. "You must be Noah. Paige should be down any minute.

Can I take your jacket?"

Noah was still in the foyer taking off his jacket as Paige came down the stairs. "Hi, Noah. Would you like a Coke?" she asked, leading him into the living room.

I'll get it. You two just go ahead and visit," Heather said as she went to the kitchen.

Noah stood at the doorway of the living room looking at all the books that lined the wall. "Wow! You could open a library with all these books. Have you read them all?"

"My dad is the avid reader. I guess I inherited my interest in books from him."

"What does your dad do for a living?" he asked.

She looked away from the books and turned to Noah. "Enough about my family; I want to know more about you. Let's see—you like to collect things off the beach, you work with your uncle, and you definitely have a talent in building sand castles. I know you live about an hour from here— Rune Drive, right?"

"Actually, it's called Rune Ridge Way. It's off Warwick Road."

Paige stood by the couch and motioned for him to have a seat. "Have you lived there long?"

"Well, to be honest, my uncle owns many different places. We visit this area a couple times a year. I don't get out much, and when I do, I like to go to the beach. I'm pretty much a loner."

She laughed. "It didn't look like that on the beach."

Noah was quick to reply. "You mean those guys I was making sand castles with? They asked if they could join me. I didn't mind—the more the merrier—but when I saw you collecting shells and stuff, I thought, 'Here's someone who enjoys the same things I do. Maybe we could find treasures together.' Oh, speaking of treasures, here's the stone I promised to bring."

Noah was taking the stone out of his jacket pocket when Heather came in with some chips and Cokes. Paige thanked her mom as she took the tray.

"I'll trade you this stone for a Coke," Noah said, taking the Coke from her and putting his stone on the tray.

"I see you've brought Paige a rock off the beach. You must have noticed that she loves to collect things," Heather said, handing Noah the bowl of chips.

"Mom, do you mind?" Paige asked, hinting for Heather to leave.

She got the message and turned to leave. "I'll be in the kitchen if you need me."

Noah took the stone back off the tray and dunked it into his Coke.

"Eww! How disgusting! Why did you do that?" Paige asked.

"No big deal. It's washed." He took the stone out of his Coke and held it up to the light. "See the beautiful lacing? I can't say for sure if this is a black agate or not, but you're welcome to it."

"You're giving me your stone?"

"On one condition: if you stop being so nervous around me."

"What can I say?" Paige smiled as she looked up at Noah.

"Say nothing; it's a gift." The clock in the living room chimed. "Oh gosh, it's already eleven p.m. I hope your mother doesn't mind I'm here so late. Maybe I should go. Can I see you tomorrow?"

"I can't tomorrow. I'm leaving to visit my grandmother, remember? When I get back we can get together."

Noah winked at Paige. "Well then, I guess I'll have to wait until you get back."

She walked him to the front door and handed him his jacket. "Thanks, Noah. I promise to call you as soon as I get back."

He said his good-bye, and she watched as he walked down the porch steps and got into his car. What a day, she thought. First Noah, then Grandma, and now the black agate. Who would've thought?

CHAPTER 10

GRANDMA MORWENNA

Paige glanced down at her watch, probably for the hundredth time in the last hour, and wondered if this flight would ever end. Their arrival to Chicago had been delayed due to fog, and Paige had to listen to her mother's instructions about what she could or couldn't do while at her grandmother's and her complaints about how she might miss her connecting flight to Ireland.

The plane finally landed, and Heather gave Paige a quick hug and kiss good-bye. Before they raced to get their connecting flights, she gave Paige her last instruction: "Remember what I said, Paige. I will, see you when you get back."

"Okay mother." Paige almost missed her connection due to her mother's continued instructions, but found relief from her mother's jibber gabber on the last leg of her trip to grandmothers.

After Paige landed, she went straight to the baggage claim. The only one there was a petite, gray-haired man wearing a green plaid vest and gray pants that were gathered at his knees. He held a poster with **"PAIGE"** written in big black letters. Paige laughed and shook her head when she saw the little man; she knew it couldn't be anyone other than her grandmother who would have arranged such a driver.

"You must be Paige," the little man said as Paige approached. "I'm an old friend of your grandmother's. Here, let me help you with your luggage."

Inside the taxi, the desire to know what had been going on with her grandmother over the years gave Paige the unusual need to question the driver nonstop. She wanted to know how long he knew her grandmother, and if she was doing well. She asked him if her grandmother still had her beautiful gardens filled with herbs, flowers, and vegetables. She couldn't stop until the question burning inside of her came out: "Did my grandmother ever share any of her wonderful adventure stories with you?"

The driver smiled and laughed. "Oh, the stories your grandmother can tell. But why don't you ask her yourself?"

Paige was so busy talking that she hadn't even realized they had pulled into her grandmother's driveway. She looked out the window, and she could see all the beautiful gardens she remembered from her childhood. The old swing and rocker still hung on the front porch, and by the front door her beloved grandmother waited for her.

Morwenna was only 4'11" tall, and her long white hair was always braided into one thick braid that she swirled into a bun at the back of her head and pinned with seven small rhinestone butterfly barrettes. Her brown skirt met her ankles and covered most of a pair of black shoes that laced up to mid-calf. Her white lace blouse covered everything from neck to waist, leaving only the warmth of her rosy cheeks, big smile, and blue eyes in view.

The driver helped Paige with her luggage and greeted Morwenna as if she were royalty. He bowed, smiled, and said, "It's my pleasure to bring you your granddaughter, my queen."

Perplexed, Paige grabbed onto Morwenna's arm as she led her into the house. She gaped in awe as she went inside; nothing had changed. The wooden floor of the breezeway had the same colorful rug with fairies dancing in the forest by the light of the moon. On the left side of the entrance, French doors opened to the living room, where Paige stood in amazement.

The room had the same lavish red velvet curtains that draped across the top of the bay windows and down to the floor. Each curtain was tied back with a thick gold rope to allow the sun's rays to reflect color off the huge crystal chandelier. The east wall had walnut panels with flowers hand-carved into them, while the west wall was devoted to well-stocked bookcases. From the floor to the top of the twelve-foot ceiling, each bookcase had beveled glass doors.

Morwenna had her usual fire going in the living room. The fireplace was built from the fieldstone around her property. Every unique stone was covered in moss, which she misted regularly so it wouldn't die. An antique clock decorated the center of the mantel, and amazingly, it kept perfect time.

"Are you just going to stand there with your mouth open?" she finally asked.

Paige grinned. "Grandma, nothing has changed—not even you."

"I'm too old to change." Morwenna took a few steps back. "Now let me look at you. I can't believe it; you're a young woman now. I bet you're tired and hungry after your long flight. If you want to rest—"

"I'm too excited to lie down," Paige said. "I have so much to tell you, and I won't be here long."

"I know, dear. We'll have plenty of time over dinner. I thought we could go down to the river since tonight's the harvest moon."

"Harvest moon! Tonight? But I thought a harvest moon doesn't occur until after the autumnal equinox…oh never mind. Do I still have the same bedroom?"

"Yes dear. Everything is still the same as you left it."

"I won't be long. I can't wait for you to see the surprise I brought you, Grandma."

She kissed Morwenna, grabbed her suitcase, and ran upstairs to change into a pair of jeans and sweatshirt. She retrieved the black agate out of her luggage and placed it in her pocket for safekeeping. As she looked into the mirror and combed her hair, she smiled. I can't wait to see Grandma's reaction when I show her the black agate. Finally, we can bring Dad home.

CHAPTER 11

HARVEST MOON

Morwenna waited for Paige at the bottom of the stairs with a picnic basket and a blanket in her arms. "Are you ready to go to the river of Erainna?" she asked as Paige came down the stairs.

Paige grinned from ear to ear. "Never been readier."

Morwenna handed her the basket full of fresh-baked bread, fried chicken, and garden fresh vegetables. "Do you remember the way?"

"I would never forget the way to our special place, Grandma."

"Then lead on, my Autumn Mist."

Morwenna and Paige laughed and sang as they trotted through the wooded path that led to the river of Erainna. It wasn't long before they stopped in front of an old willow tree.

"I don't believe it," Paige said in amazement, touching the willow.

"Don't believe what, child?"

"This old willow; it's still here. Wonderful memories have been made while under this old tree. How old is this tree anyway?"

"I'm not sure. It was old when I was young." She laughed as she spread out the blanket under the tree.

Paige sat down beside her. "It's so good to be back, Grandma. I wanted to come back so many times, but Mom wouldn't listen. I'm surprised she even allowed me to come now."

Morwenna smiled as she took items from the basket and placed them on the blanket. "I'm not."

"You're not?"

"Let's just say I had a little hand in getting your mother that promotion and getting you here."

"Okay, Grandma, let's say you did get Mom that promotion, but if I hadn't asked her to call you, I wouldn't be here."

"That's true, dear. We have Otter to thank for that. By the way, a bird friend of Otter told me, that Otter wanted me to know you have a new friend. I believe Otter told him, his name is…Noah?"

"Otter told you about Noah?" she asked, surprised. "Oh, it doesn't matter, Grandma. If I had to describe Noah to you, I would say he's charming, tall, and really built, but his eyes…it was his eyes that took my breath away. They're the most beautiful blue in the entire world. I can't explain it, but his kindness, even after I was so rude to him, made his eyes even more beautiful. Noah had something I was looking for, and he just gave it to me." She pulled the black agate out of her pocket, excited to show it to Morwenna at last. "Look, Grandma, the black agate."

"Otter told me you thought Noah had it." She took the stone and held it up for the moon to shine its bright light onto it, reminding Paige of the way Noah had held it up to the light in her living room, but the moon withheld its reflection.

"Isn't it beautiful?" Paige asked as Morwenna studied the stone.

"I'm sure you find it quite beautiful, but it's not what you want," she said and raised her hand to toss the stone into the river.

Paige grabbed her hand. "Don't!"

"Autumn Mist, it's not the agate. This thing is a cursed stone; it will bring you nothing but harm."

"Cursed?"

Morwenna took hold of her hand and led her closer to the river's bank. "Listen to me. I want you to look into the river and tell me what you see."

"I see the moon's reflection, and some of the stars glittering. So what?"

"That's all?"

"Yes. What else is there to see?"

"My dear, maybe you should sit down. This may take a while. Before your father left…." She paused to compose herself. "Before he left, he too had a stone he thought was the black agate. He didn't believe me when I told him it was not the right stone. He grabbed it out of my hand before I could stop him." Morwenna took Paige by the hand. "Autumn

Mist, think about it. Do you think I would toss this stone into the river if I thought for one moment it was the black agate?"

"No," she mumbled.

"I miss your father. I'm not getting any younger, and more than anything, I want to see him before I leave this life. Believe me, this is not the black agate. It's cursed. Just look into the water and trust me. If you really want to help your father, you'll have to listen to me. Let me toss the stone into the river, then look into the water."

"Okay, Grandma, I'll do as you say. But I'm scared. What happens if this is the right stone that could bring Dad home?"

"Just trust me. Let me toss the stone into the water." Paige took in a deep breath and let go of her hand. She watched the stone splash into the river, then looked into the water as Morwenna instructed. "I can't see anything, Grandma. What am I supposed to see?"

"Look beyond the surface."

"Grandma, I don't see…wait, I hear something—faint voices." The bright yellow moon turned blood red as small flashes of light rose out of the water. Paige didn't move a muscle when the flashes fluttered toward the sky.

"Look into the water, Autumn Mist, and tell me what you see."

Paige strained her eyes so she could focus deeper into the water. "I see seahorses, Grandma! But how could seahorses be in a river? It doesn't make sense."

"Do you see anything else unusual about the seahorses?"

"That's odd. They all have human faces. Dad!" Paige screamed as she started to fall into the river.

"No!" Morwenna cried as a vine from the willow tree grabbed Paige's arm so she couldn't fall into the water. "Vindamar's curse stone took my son, but I won't let it get my granddaughter."

Paige turned toward her grandmother's voice. "Grandma, you're… you're…"

"A willow tree! I changed so I could grab you before you went into the water. I opened the porthole to Zandora so you wouldn't fall into the water."

Paige's mouth stayed opened and continued to speak. "But…she gulped. "It's been so long since I've been here, I thought this place was a dream I made up from the stories you told. And what about the seahorses—they look like they have…"

"Human faces?"

"Yes."

"You see, those seahorses are Zandorians, and humans too; they are under Vindamar's spell to look like Undines."

"Undines—so Dad is an Undine?"

"Yes. I wanted you to know what happened to him before I die. He loves you so much; he didn't want you to meet the same fate he did. I wanted to explain some things before I opened the porthole and brought you here to Zandoria."

Paige looked back at the river, "So this is what happened to Dad. Where did he go?" she asked, trying to spot her father.

"Every time a cursed stone is tossed into the river, they come to the surface to greet the person who falls in. Then they go back into the depths of the river. Look, Autumn Mist, Vindamar is getting stronger now that he has the dewdrop crystal. The only way to bring your father home is to break the spell Vindamar has on him, and to do that, the dewdrop crystal must be placed back in the meadow of Amaranth."

"Wait—I thought Dad needed the black agate, not some dewdrop crystal."

"We really need both. The black agate gives us power and strength over Vindamar, but without the dewdrop crystal, we won't survive much longer. That crystal provides the dew that sings and supplies life to all things. You see, my child, Vindamar may have control over the Zandorians right now, but he doesn't hold the same power over you."

"Why not?"

Still part of a willow tree, Morwenna looked deeply into her eyes. "Vindamar doesn't know that I have something very dear to him. It is the one thing that has stopped him from becoming all-powerful. A gold coin."

"A coin?"

She hesitated, and then seemed to reach a decision. "My dear, you will be eighteen soon. We all tried to protect you— your mother, father, and even I did—by keeping certain information from you, but it's time that you know the truth.

Come and sit, for the night is young, and the secret you are about to hear will take a while to tell."

CHAPTER 12

THE BEGINNING OF THE LEGEND

(Morwenna's Story)

Paige remembered from her childhood that when her grandmother said, "It will take a while," she should sit down. She made herself comfortable on the blanket, faced her grandmother, and waited for her to begin.

"I am Morwenna, one of only a handful of Zandorians left. I come from a time when sorcerers like Merlin walked this earth."

"Wait—you're telling me you lived in Merlin's time?"

"Autumn Mist, please don't interrupt."

"Sorry, Grandma."

"Merlin wasn't the only sorcerer around. Even though he was very powerful, he had a formidable adversary named Vindamar, the first-born to King Torin. Vindamar's demeanor and looks were far different from the other carefree Andalarians; his eyes held the emptiness of the great white shark. It wasn't his gigantic frame that frightened the Andalarians or the Zandorians, but his deep, harsh voice. It brought chills to their bones. To make things worse, his disregard for life left him ruthless. He misused his birthright to crush the weak and mild-mannered souls. It was, as Vindamar put it, his birthright and obligation to decide what should live or die.

"To Vindamar, people were only puppets to fulfill to his wishes, to increase his evil powers, which brought him control over the universe. His powers grew as people brought suffering upon each other with their thievery, deceit, selfishness, and hatred for one another. These actions robbed and depleted the universe of its gifts of love, plants, animals, and the water. Vindamar knew without love all would lose hope; without plants there was no medicine for the caregivers to heal; without bees there wouldn't be pollination for food; and without water all would perish.

"However, there was hope through Malachi, second son of King Torin. His eyes were blue as the sea and filled with kindness. Malachi's heart brought warmth to everyone he touched. When he reached manhood, he married his longtime sweetheart Amaranth, and they had a son. Together they worked to bring happiness to everyone they encountered and brought justice to the helpless. They labored in fields so others had food when it was scarce. They showed kindness and patience in a time of discord, for Malachi and his family believed in something other than serving themselves. They were the daydreamers who saw beyond the stars, walked with creatures' great and small, and believed in creation that science could not explain.

"Malachi loved his brother, so he did not want to oppose Vindamar's cruelty, but King Torin knew if there was to be stability, hope, and life in the land after he died, Malachi must be king, not Vindamar.

"As Vindamar's powers became stronger, King Torin knew something had to be done and soon, for his health was failing him. He sent out one of his trusted kinsmen to deliver a message to his dear friend Merlin, who had predicted Vindamar's rise in power and the birth of the one who could stop him—a maiden born of Zandorian and mortal blood. He called a secret meeting with Malachi and some of his other trusted kinsmen. King Torin had the kinsmen witness the transfer of the gold coin to Malachi, which entitled him to the throne. Vindamar received word from Catigern, a bat he put a spell on, that his father had selected Malachi to receive the gold coin. Infuriated, he raced to his father to see if it was true. With King Torin's nod of confirmation, Vindamar was overtaken by rage. He drew his sword and, with one blow, killed his father, then left to find Malachi."

Morwenna paused in her story, but Paige was eager to hear more. "What happened next?"

"Well, Malachi knew Vindamar would know he had the gold coin. Afraid for his son's safety, Malachi secretly met with me and entrusted the coin to me. His fear proved to be true; when Malachi returned to his castle and denied Vindamar the coin, Vindamar tortured him. Enraged that Malachi didn't waver, he had Amaranth brought in to watch Malachi suffer. She pleaded with Vindamar to let them go, but he only laughed and mocked her. He grew tired of her pleas and killed her, making Malachi witness it before he took Malachi's life. Before he left the castle, he went to his nephew's room and yanked the two-year-old out of his bed.

Then he disappeared, taking the boy to the meadows of Amaranth. There he took the dewdrop crystal that gave life to the Zandorian inhabitants. Not only did Vindamar get our crystal, but he also succeeded in getting the red agate."

"Wait, I thought the agate was black."

"I'll get to that—Vindamar hoped by taking the agate that it would lead him to the gold coin, leaving the kingdom weak and him as king.

"Merlin had arrived with King Torin's kinsmen too late. Unable to change what had been done, and knowing he wouldn't see justice for it in his lifetime, he placed a spell on the kingdom of Zandora. Under this spell, Merlin's closest and most trusted friends never aged like the other Andalarians and Zandorians, and King Torin's only grandchild would never age beyond twenty. Merlin also called upon the king's kinsmen, who had drafted the laws between Zandora, mortals, and the different worlds to form the new world's legion. These kinsmen agreed to have Merlin place a spell over them that would allow them to live beyond their natural years so they could protect the grandson of King Torin and the maiden who would be born from the blood of different worlds.

"Merlin knew the extent of Vindamar's powers and had the foresight to know that Vindamar would eventually find out what had been discussed behind those closed doors. He needed to protect the throne of King Torin, and he needed a way to outwit Vindamar. He allowed only parts of what happened in that meeting be known to only a handful of kinsmen, and he met separately and in secrecy with only the closest and strongest of King Torin's kinsmen.

"The agreement was to go ahead and tell the world about the maiden who would bring peace and prosperity—for everyone needed to have hope—but one part that was never revealed was that the kinsmen who agreed to protect the land and its inhabitants were also the decoys. They were willing to give up their lives for the ones who would actually protect the maiden and King Torin's grandson.

"And the other part that was never revealed was that the protectors of the maiden also had the ability to change their appearance in case Vindamar discovered who they were.

"Those of us who took this oath knew we would live long enough to see the maiden, but we also knew it would be left in the hands of the maiden whether she would accept the challenge that lay before her."

Morwenna's story seemed to be winding down now, and Paige stared at her, dumbfounded. She had never told a story quite like this. "Grandma, why are you telling me all this?"

"Autumn Mist, your father is Zandorian, and your mother is mortal. Do you understand now?"

She rose from the blanket and began to pace nervously. "If you're trying to say that I'm the maiden, you're wrong. It's only a story."

"No, it's not just a story. I was a friend of Merlin alongside King Torin. It was by Merlin's powers that I was given the responsibility of keeping the Zandorians and other inhabitants of this dimension safe."

"Mom is right. You are crazy if you think I'm the maiden." She didn't want to believe it of her beloved grandmother, but she didn't know what else to think.

"For someone who is speaking to a talking willow tree in another dimension, and doesn't find it odd that she can talk to animals, I'm not sure who is crazier. Autumn Mist—"

"This can't be happening!" Paige screamed.

"Look at me, Autumn Mist."

Paige looked at her for a few moments. "Okay, Grandma, maybe it's true about Dad—even Merlin—but you're wrong about me. I'm not the maiden everyone is hoping for."

"You must hear me out. It was said that after Vindamar killed his brother, he stole the red agate. He hoped that by taking the agate that gave the Zandorians their strength over him; they would tell him the whereabouts of the gold coin. When that didn't work, his anger got the best of him, and he placed an evil spell on the agate to weaken the Zandorians. The spell became a cancer to the stone and changed the color from red to black. Word has it, Vindamar traveled far to toss the agate into a great lake and then went after the dewdrop crystal.

"The Zandorian inhabitants believe that the black agate will wash up when it is time for the maiden to reclaim it. Merlin said the maiden would find the agate, but he also said it would take a mighty battle for the agate to be reclaimed. I believe Vindamar still has the agate; even with a temper as foul as Vindamar's, he wouldn't toss that agate out. He knows its value.

"Autumn Mist, the day you were born, your father and I knew your fate. We both saw the small red dewdrop on your forehead, which was foretold by Merlin. We never spoke of it or told anyone for your own safety. Your father knew the legend and understood what we saw. The problem he had was thinking that he could change your destiny.

"He believed that if he could find the black agate first, he could spare you from Vindamar's grip. He couldn't endure the thought of losing you, but it was the only outcome he could see. He knew time was running out for us all, because the dewdrop crystal sings to supply life, and Vindamar won't let it sing. This imbalance here caused a lack of water for us all, and as you know, all living things need water.

"Your father's plan was to keep Vindamar close to him so he could keep you and others safe. What better way to fight evil than to know what it is up to? It seemed to work for a while, but somehow Vindamar found out that your father was searching for the black agate, so he gave him a rock similar to the one you had. Your father was certain it was the black agate, and he tried to place a spell on Vindamar, but it backfired and turned him into a seahorse. It almost happened to you. It would have if I hadn't stepped in. Trust me, Autumn Mist, Vindamar can't find out who you are. If he does, he will destroy you."

CHAPTER 13

UNVEILING THE COIN

Morwenna looked out over the river and fell very silent as she bowed her head. "My heart has been broken ever since I lost your father. Without the crystal I can't even cry tears over my loss."

Paige just stood there without saying a word. She wasn't sure what to think or how she felt about any of this, but she knew that if she wanted to get her father back, she had to do something. "Grandma, you said I'm the maiden. Tell me how I can get the crystal so I can take on Vindamar."

"I'm not sure if I can let you go. How could I expect you to take on Vindamar when you haven't even had a job yet? To get the crystal from Vindamar, one must be smarter and stronger than he is. And even if you do manage to make it to his castle, it will take an army to defeat him. I don't know, Autumn Mist. I promised your mother and father I would watch over you."

Paige stood up and paced for a couple of minutes before she went over to her grandmother. "I know I can do this. I'm strong and determined. Together, we can put Vindamar where he belongs, back in the bottomless pit he came out of, but I can't do this alone. Will you help me, Grandma?"

Morwenna studied her for a very long time. "Are you sure you're ready?"

"I've got to do it, with or without you."

"You're just like your father, but you have an advantage over Vindamar that he didn't. Vindamar knew your father, and he knows about the maiden, but he doesn't know who the maiden is Autumn

Mist. If you go on this quest, you'll find more enemies than friends. Many have no choice but to follow Vindamar, for he can cast spells to make people do his bidding. His powers have become stronger with each passing day."

She paused to let her words soak in, and then she continued. "I know you're determined to help your father, so I must help you. It's very important that you remember what I'm about to tell you. First of all, always use the name Paige. I gave you the name Autumn Jorah Mist for a reason. It is symbolic to Vindamar. Autumn means harvest, which reminds him of his brother. Mist is for the dewdrop crystal he took from the Zandorians, and Jorah means rain. He despises anything that is good in this world. Rain brings life, and that is the last thing he wants. When you meet Vindamar, he will call you Autumn Mist, but you won't hear Jorah, for it is a Biblical name. If Vindamar ever finds out that you are Autumn Jorah Mist, he will destroy you.

"Second, you need to find Mela the gray wolf. She hides out in the woods of Lindera—the place where you and your father used to pick blueberries. Find Mela, and she'll be your guide in finding Vindamar's castle. Listen to and watch Mela, for she is very smart and has many friends who will assist you. There will be a time when she can't continue, for she has young pups to watch over. She knows that as long as she doesn't enter Vindamar's dwelling, he can't touch her."

Morwenna lifted one of her roots from the muddy ground. "I want you to grab hold of this root and break it off. You will need a staff to help you along the way."

Paige took hold of the root with both hands and placed one foot near the trunk of the tree. She tugged on the root until she broke off a piece long enough to use as a walking stick.

"Good. Now place it on the ground and stand back," said Morwenna, and she started to chant. "Htiw eht pleh fo ruo rotaerc siht ffats llahs gnirb ecitsuj morf eht ecitsujni."

It became dark as the clouds covered the moon. The earth shook as a bolt of lightning came out of the darkness and struck the staff. After a few moments, the earth stopped shaking, and the embers on the staff died out. The clouds that had covered the moon finally parted, and Morwenna returned to the grandmother form that Paige knew and loved. Morwenna picked up the staff and dipped it into the river before she handed it to Paige.

Paige strained her eyes to get a closer look at her staff. "Grandma, you're unbelievable! It has some type of engraving on it—is that the moon and stars?" She went on without waiting for an answer. "And over here it looks like the animals are talking to a person. What does all of this mean?"

"The answers will come in due time, Autumn Mist. The spell I've placed on your staff will help you when you need it. Anyone with good intentions will notice the symbols and help you, but beware of anyone or anything that does not recognize your staff, for they come with an evil heart."

Paige held her staff up so the moon's light could shine on it. "Can I do magic spells with it?"

"Yes, but the spell I put on this staff is not as strong as I would like it to be. It should keep us connected. When you need me, all you need to do is raise your staff and call out my name, but realize that I won't be able to help you once you leave the forest of Lindera. My powers have weakened as Vindamar's powers have become stronger."

"Vindamar has nothing on you, Grandma."

"You must take Vindamar's powers seriously. If you don't understand what I'm saying then you will have to give up this notion of helping your father. It's important to stay focused; concentrate on what I'm saying. There will be many days and times on your journey that you will feel alone. Promise me you will always know that I am with you, especially when your hardships are unbearable. You must promise me you will never forget this."

Paige rubbed the symbols on her staff. "I promise."

"You don't have to go, Autumn Mist. You can stay here and forget everything I have told you and go on with your life as a mortal. Your family loves you whether you go on this journey or stay home."

Morwenna pulled her into her arms and held her tight, and Paige felt sadness overwhelm her. She had the same knots of emptiness in her stomach as when her father disappeared, but she had to stay focused, just as Morwenna had said. She pushed away from her. "Don't worry. With this staff, I know I'll make it."

"My dear, before you leave, there's one more thing I want you to have." Morwenna took something muddy out of her pocket and placed it in Paige's right hand. "This is the coin Vindamar wants but doesn't know I have. I've kept this coin a secret, hidden away in the roots of the willow tree. I was to keep it safe and out of Vindamar's hands at all costs. An oath was made to ensure that the coin you now hold was given to you when the time was right. That coin is your birthright; it is the last gift a mighty king had to offer for the survival of his kingdom and ours."

"What do you mean it's my birthright?"

"I am the Queen of Zandora because I was given the coin, Your father—my son—would be next in line for the throne, but he is under Vindamar's spell. Under the laws and treaty of the legion, this makes you the next in line. But without this coin, the throne will not be yours."

"You're the queen; why don't you keep the coin?"

"It does not belong to me; it belongs to you. There are two others who could claim that coin: one is Vindamar, and the other is King Torin's grandson, the boy Vindamar took from Malachi's castle."

"How can one coin change the world?"

"The coin holds the power over many kingdoms, and its bearer embraces not only the throne but also the right to balance life over all. That coin has the power to be used for good, but in the wrong hands, it is also the root of evil that could destroy this land. Vindamar needs it to hold the throne to the different kingdoms. He has killed for less and will stop at nothing to get it.

Let me make it clear, Autumn Mist: do not show the coin to anyone. It is the only thing keeping your father and others alive. If Vindamar gets it, your father will die, and life as we know it will end. It is better to give up your life than to allow the coin to end up in Vindamar's hands. I'm sorry you'll have to go on this journey with no other provisions from me other than the staff I have given you. You will have to use your wits and the friends you meet along the way. Don't forget. Paige is your only name. Find Mela. But most of all take care of that coin."

Feeling the weight of the quest before her, Paige tucked the coin safely in her pocket, and without a word she turned toward the woods where she used to collect blueberries with her father. The desire to retreat into her grandmother's arms was so strong that she dared not turn around and look at her one last time.

As she walked away, Morwenna whispered blessings into the wind. "So the prophecy begins, Autumn Mist. May the Creator keep you safe and give you the wisdom and strength you will need on your journey. Let your journey begin, my Autumn Mist."

CHAPTER 14

THE JOURNEY BEGINS

About an hour into Paige's journey she stopped to listen for the beautiful birdsong that once filled the air, but the birds no longer sang. Most of the oak, maple, and elm trees that had thrived when she and her father had come here were now dead or on the verge of dying. The lush, green wild grasses that housed butterflies, rabbits, and many other small animals had dried to brown straw. Even the moon no longer illuminated the path they had taken so many times before his disappearance. Though things had changed for the worse, Paige walked on. The only time she stopped was to either catch her breath or glance around to get her bearings.

Suddenly she heard twigs snapping close by, and she fell almost as still as a statue. Her eyes swept her surroundings, searching for signs of an enemy. A chill ran down her spine while a breeze swept her hair away from her neck. Finally, she placed both hands over her heart and took in a deep breath. The only thing she heard now was the pounding of her own heart. It was probably some raccoon or skunk, she thought. *I can't let every little noise bother me, or I'll never get to Mela.*

She clutched her staff closer to her side and patted the right pocket of her jeans where she stashed the gold coin. She stopped periodically to glance around while she listened for sounds that didn't fit the rhythm of her steps. Nervously, she started to hum, but was interrupted by the rustling of bushes. "I hear you behind those bushes. Come out and show yourself!" she demanded.

From behind the shrubbery, two large warthogs appeared and blocked the path Paige traveled. They looked at each other, and then at

50

her. "Who are you, and what are you doing in the woods of Amyrha?" asked one of the warthogs.

Before Paige could answer, the warthog turned and whispered to his friend, "Hey, isn't that the girl Noah met on the beach?"

"If you have something to say to me, you shouldn't whisper. It's rude. I can't answer your questions if I can't hear what you are asking."

She looked at the first warthog, "In answer to your question, my name is Paige, and I'm lost. I've been traveling for hours and can't find my way out." She took a few steps backward as the warthogs approached.

"Aww, did you hear that, Sam? She's lost. Too bad for you, missy, but it's our lucky day. Let's get her, Sam!"

"I don't know, Jake. She looks like she wants us to chase her."

As the warthogs slowly approached Paige, she stood her ground and thought about her grandmother's words: When you need me, all you need to do is raise your staff and call out my name. Paige pointed the staff toward the warthogs and yelled, "Morwenna!"

The wind instantly turned violent, scooping up dirt and debris. Thunder rumbled, and Paige heard words spew out of her mouth in a language she didn't know: "Sha hi im lor be gu ton."

Just as the warthogs were about to reach Paige, a blinding bolt of lightning hit the ground. It wasn't until the dust settled and the lightning stopped that she was able to see. There on the ground, where the two warthogs had stood, were two piles of black cinders. Shaken by the incident, Paige dropped to her knees, trembling. For the first time since her father's disappearance, she was able to produce a tear.

CHAPTER 15

BOTTOMLESS PIT TO MOUNTAIN PEAKS

It was several minutes before Paige could compose herself enough to stand. She scraped the dirt off her jeans and drifted further into the merciless wood. In its never-ending darkness, she ran into tree branches that at times tangled in her hair. She tripped over limbs and small boulders.

Exhausted, she leaned against a tree trunk. Maybe I should stop. No, I can't. The sooner I find Mela, the sooner I'll find Dad. How much farther can it be to Mela's den?

She forced herself to go on. She stumbled through the endless carpet of dead leaves, rotten plants, and unforeseen dangers. Paige took another step and felt the ground give. She found herself engulfed in what she thought was a sticky mud pit, but the more she struggled to free herself, the faster she sank. She was unable to move her legs as easily.

Quicksand! She managed to raise her staff into the air and called out, "Morwenna!" She waited a couple of seconds for her grandmother to rescue her. When nothing happened, she called out again, "Morwenna!" She struggled to keep her head and hands above the quicksand. Almost completely submerged, she tilted her head back to keep the quicksand from running into her mouth. Again she cried out, "Morwenna, where are you? Please, I need help!"

As the quicksand engulfed her, she tried to move very slowly to the edge of the pit, but the watery muck started to seep into her mouth. She coughed up the gritty liquid and shouted once more. "Grandma, I—"

With unfinished words, Paige went under. All fell silent as she sank into the bottomless pit; only her hands were visible as she clutched the staff that her grandmother had given her.

Woosh…Woosh…Woosh…disrupted the eerie silence that fell over the woods of Amyrha. Unknown to Paige it was the resonance of the enormous fifteen-foot wingspan of a dragon approaching.

Swiftly he swooped down and grabbed the staff Paige held onto. She clung to her staff as she felt the tug lifting her out of the muddy pit. She coughed and gasped for air.

"Thank you, Grandma. I was almost out of air. I knew you wouldn't let me down."

As the dragon flew higher and higher, Paige realized the sky was growing lighter. As they soared above the mountain peaks, the sun's rays beamed into daylight.

Cold and wet, Paige shivered uncontrollably though the sun brought warmth. "Grandma!" she yelled. "I'm getting weak. You must find a place to let me down." She tried desperately to maintain her grip on the staff, but her arms and hands gave out, and she found herself free falling to the ground. The creature let go of the staff, and like an eagle after a fish, dove for her and caught her.

Unable to look up, Paige floundered in the creature's grip. The dragon carried Paige to the mountain of Brielle and dropped her in a nest built on a ledge next to a waterfall.

The nest was built from large branches of dead trees held together with mud, and because it was lined with lush green moss and ferns which were thriving from the waterfall's mist, it cushioned her fall. The last thing Paige saw before she closed her eyes was the dragon as it circled and then disappeared.

For several hours, Paige lay motionless, napping in the comfort of the moss before she sat up. With her eyes now wide open, she turned her head from side to side and pulled her knees close to her chest. Where am I?

Alert, she stood and brushed off her clothes, and then she reached eagerly for the waterfall. She cupped her hands together and gathered enough water to wash most off the quicksand from her face and hands before she took a few sips. Once refreshed she started to climb up the slippery wall. She tried to find hand and footholds in the mossy mountainside, but every time she tried to pull herself up, she lost her grip and slid back down into the nest.

She harrumphed in frustration. "Without my staff, how am I going to get out of here?" She hammered the nest's floor with her fist. Frustrated, she stood up and paced the nest, and then she spotted a vine dangling a few feet away. If I can get to that vine, and it's strong enough to hold me, I should be able to climb out of here. It took her numerous attempts and a couple of falls before she managed to get hold of the vine and climb toward the top of the nest.

She willed herself on, even though her muscles ached, her hands shook, and salty sweat burned as it dripped into her eyes. Steadily, she pulled herself upward. It wasn't until she was out of the nest and had crawled far enough from its edge that she collapsed face down on the ground. She rolled onto her back and gasped in the air, and it didn't take long before she could stand up and stretch out the kinks in her arms and shoulders.

The mountainous terrain of rocks and intertwining tree roots caused Paige to fall several times as she walked. When she stumbled again and turned to see what had caused her fall, she let out a happy squeal of, "Grandma!" It was her staff.

She hugged the staff, overwhelmed by emotion and exhaustion. Oh Grandma, I wish I were home. I could be soaking in a hot tub of water and sleeping in a comfortable bed with my fluffy pillow. I can almost smell Mom's meatloaf. "Maybe I should have listened to you,

Grandma," she said aloud. "I really didn't think this would be so hard. How am I going to do this?" But she knew it was too late to turn back. She stood up and forced herself to go on.

The sun had started to descend when Paige noticed a small opening in the roots of a massive tree. Curious, she approached the opening and peered inside. It looked like a small den capable of providing temporary shelter. "It isn't home, but it will do for the night," she decided.

Before going into the den she rubbed her stomach as it rumbled, protesting its emptiness. Not far from where she sat there was a bush filled with bluish-purple berries. She went over to the bush and picked a berry, then sniffed it before placing it into her mouth. She shuddered as her mouth puckered and her eye squinted. They're not blueberries, but they'll do. She continued to pick and eat the berries. It wasn't long before she began to sway back and forth, then she dropped to the ground. Unable to move, Paige looked over to where her staff lay only inches out of reach.

Darkness fell around her and she still couldn't move. Just a few feet from where she lay, two eyes reflected the moonlight. "Who are you?" she mumbled before her eyes closed.

CHAPTER 16
ATWOOD

Night passed, and though Paige was burning with fever and lay directly in the sun's rays, she had stopped sweating. She found her mouth was dry, and she was sick to her stomach. She managed to roll herself onto her side, and then she slowly sat up.

What happened? She rubbed her forehead. *The last thing I remember was eating some berries and falling to the ground.* She tried to stand and quickly became dizzy, which forced her to sit back down. *I shouldn't have eaten those berries.*

She crawled back to her staff. "Grandma, what should I do? I'm too sick and dehydrated to find Mela."

"Mela?" a strange voice asked.

She looked around, trying to locate the voice, and saw nothing. "Who's there?"

"Well," the voice said, "it depends on who's asking. You said something about Mela, and you hold a staff from our queen." A red fox came out from under a large root.

"Am I hallucinating, or are you really there?"

"You're not hallucinating. I'm real. How did you obtain the queen's staff?" the fox asked.

"I'm Paige, and your queen gave me this to help me on my quest."

"Nice to meet you, Paige. My name is Atwood. You say you're on a quest. What quest?"

"Well, I guess I can tell you—you did recognize the queen's staff, as you called it. I have to find Vindamar."

"Vindamar! Why in the world would you want to find him?"

"I'm sorry, Atwood, but that's between Mela, Vindamar, and me. I could really use your help in finding Mela." Paige bent over and grabbed her stomach.

"I'll tell you what, Paige. I'll go to Mela and see if she will allow a visit, but in the meantime, you need to get out of this sun. You've eaten muddle berries; they're deadly to mortals if not treated properly. I take it, since you're still alive, you're not mortal."

"Well, sort of. I'm part mortal."

The fox rubbed his chin with his paw. "Hmm…part mortal? This means you're going to get worse before you get better, and if you don't get treatment for the poison you've ingested, you won't get better at all. The first thing you need to do is get out of the sun. You can stay with me; I'll help you get inside my house. Once you're out of the sun, I can go and gather some ginger root and other herbs for you to take. If I don't hurry, you'll be gone before nightfall, and I can't have that now, can I?"

Atwood helped Paige crawl under the tree roots. "You can rest here. I'll be back with some ginger root and water." Atwood turned and took off, leaving Paige by herself once more. When he returned, she was asleep. He set to work, crushing the ginger root and other herbs together in a large shell and mixing them with some water. Once completed, Atwood took his mixture to Paige's side. "Here, Paige, sip this." Unable to move, she blinked a couple of times at Atwood.

"Oh my, somehow I need to get this into you, and soon." Atwood said.

Paige lay helpless as he placed the mixture closer to her lips. "I know it's hard, Paige, but you must open your mouth, even if it's just a little. If you don't try, I can't get this remedy into you to fight off the poison."

But Paige simply couldn't get her mouth to open. "Don't worry," he said. "I have another idea. I'll be right back."

Atwood left Paige's side and went outside. A few minutes later, he returned with some porcupine quills and filled one of the hollow quills with some of the remedy. With his paws he carefully placed the quill between her lips, and little by little the medicine trickled between her lips and into her mouth. After a few applications, she began to feel some relief from the pain and nausea. She gladly drifted back into sleep.

Atwood stayed by her side, filling the porcupine quill with his remedy and dripping the mixture between her lips. He also covered her with ferns when she shivered, and wiped off her brow as she sweated out the poison. Many days passed, and Paige still hadn't regained consciousness. Atwood vowed to stay by her side for as long as she needed him, though exhaustion was beginning to take its toll. Just as his eyes drifted shut, he heard a tiny voice.

"What time is it?" Paige asked as she tried to sit up.

"You're awake!" he rejoiced. "Who cares about the time? What really matters is you're going to be okay." He yipped and danced around her bed.

She glanced around. "How long have I been sleeping?"

"Eight nights."

"Eight!" she squeaked. "I have to find Mela."

"You're very weak. You must rest, my princess."

Paige stared at him. "Who told you I'm a princess?"

"I had my suspicions when I saw you with the queen's staff. I wasn't sure who you were until I started to put things together—the staff, being part mortal—but then a gold coin fell out of your pocket."

Paige felt her pants pocket and realized in horror that the gold coin was missing.

Atwood went to a picture hanging on the wall and retrieved the gold coin from behind it. "Did Morwenna tell you that this coin carries the seal of royalty and was entrusted to her by King Torin's son Malachi?"

"Grandma did say something about King Torin."

He placed the coin in her hand. "Do you know how lucky you are that one of Vindamar's thugs didn't find you? They would have killed you for that coin. You must be more careful in what you do or say. As a friend to your grandmother, I have to tell you, I'm not sure if you're ready to take this journey. You have important decisions to make, and it is imperative that you understand Vindamar cannot get his hands on this coin—under any circumstances. Vindamar's power becomes stronger when others commit evil deeds, and this coin gives him the power to rule over everything. Do you understand what I'm trying to say?"

"Grandma said the exact same thing to me, but I guess I really didn't give much thought to it. All I could think about was how I wanted my dad to come home, and I wanted to prove to my mom that Dad didn't just leave us, that Grandma's stories are true."

"I understand, Paige. Everyone who knows your grandmother knows your father's plight. I'm sure she made it very clear to you that you won't be able to save your father if Vindamar gets the coin."

Paige glanced at Atwood, then at the coin. "Then you know why I must find Vindamar?"

"Yes, I do. Who doesn't know the legend of the maiden?" He laughed.

"Then why do you laugh at me?"

"I never thought the maiden would come in my lifetime, let alone that I would have her in my home under the tree roots." He grew serious again as he continued. "Mela will be pleased that you have arrived. I promise you, Princess, we'll leave to find Mela once you get your strength back. You have to be very careful; Vindamar and his army are looking for you. I promise we will leave when you are well enough."

CHAPTER 17
MELA

Paige took Atwood's advice and stayed with him until she regained her strength. In the meantime, Atwood kept his promise to Paige and sent word to Mela that Paige wanted help on her journey to find Vindamar. Mela knew from Atwood's description that Paige was the maiden everyone had been waiting for, and that Paige was only a day away from her. Mela had no time to waste and needed to prepare her pups for her departure.

"Little ones," she called her pups close to her. "I've heard that our princess has arrived. If the rumors are true, I'll have to be away from you for a little while."

"A real princess, Mother?" asked one of the pups.

"Yes, dear, a real princess. Now I want all of you to promise me that you'll stay close to home and not go out unless you get permission from whomever I decide to take care of you. Do you understand little ones?"

"Yes, Mother," the pups said in unison.

Mela went over all the rules and the hiding places that would keep them safe. She didn't want to scare them, but she wanted to make sure they understood the rules and what they needed to do if danger came their way. Afterward, she licked each pup tenderly and promised that she would not be gone for long.

By the third day of instruction, a familiar scent approached the cave. Mela stood guard at an entrance as her pups hid. Atwood made his presence known before he entered the cave.

"Mela, it is I, Atwood. I've come with our princess."

"How are you, Atwood? Please come in." Mela bowed down in front of Paige. "My princess, please enter."

"You must be Mela. I've heard so much about you." She didn't take her eyes off Mela as she bowed in kind.

"Haven't you ever seen a wolf before?" Mela asked.

"I'm sorry, but I've never been this close to a wolf before. You're so beautiful. May I touch you?"

Mela chuckled and came closer to Paige. "If it pleases you, then go ahead."

"Wow! Your fur is so soft."

"You're a strange princess, but I'm sure you didn't come all this way just to feel my fur."

Paige withdrew her hand. "You're right; I'm here for another reason. I need your help in finding—"

"Sorry to interrupt, my princess, but I have little ones around. Do you mind if we speak outside?"

Once outside, Mela spoke openly to Paige. "I know why you're here. I will help you as much as I can, but you'll have to understand something. I can only get you as far as the outskirts of Vindamar's castle. After that, I'll only be a hindrance to you. "We don't have much time. We'll leave once my children are asleep. By then, Vindamar's spies should be back at the castle to keep him company."

One little brave pup popped his head out of the cave. "Is it safe to come out and see the princess, Mother?"

Mela laughed as she motioned with her paw for her pups to approach. "You may all come out and greet your princess. You see how fast word gets around, my princess?"

Two more pups popped their little heads out from behind a large rock, and then ran toward their mother.

"This is my firstborn, Alvar," Mela said.

"I'm the bravest," he said, puffing out his chest.

"That's not true!" another cried. "You're not the bravest! You saw Mother and decided to go to her, that's all."

"That's Loki, my second son." Mela chuckled. "He's my spokesman. And the quiet one who hides behind me is Zoë, my only girl."

"I'm quiet because a girl can't get a word in when she has two brothers," Zoë protested.

The pups huddled around their mother. "You'll have to excuse my children. They're still very young and have much to learn. Children, it's time we get inside. It will be bedtime soon, and I have many things to go over before you go to sleep."

With those words, the pups immediately went back into the cave. Mela fed and washed each pup, and before they closed their eyes, she told them a story about a mother wolf taking a princess on a long journey to faraway places. She told them that three little pups would have to be brave and strong and help a handsome fox look after them while their mother was away. She also told them how important it was that they listened to the fox and did not go outside unless the fox told them it was okay. She continued with her story until the last pup had fallen asleep.

Before Mela left, she turned to Atwood. "I've sent word to Gundar that the princess is with me and to expect us in three to five days. If you do not hear back from me or Gundar within a week, take the pups and travel east. Go high into the mountains of Orzora. You and the pups should be safe there." With everything said, Mela kissed her pups in their slumber, then left with Paige.

CHAPTER 18

MELA'S LAST BREATH

Once outside, Paige turned to Mela and asked, "Who's Gundar?"

"Gundar is a very dear friend of mine. He also knows your grandmother. He is a spider."

"A spider! We're going to meet a spider?"

"Gundar is no ordinary spider. He is one of the oldest and wisest warriors ever known. He can make himself taller than you can imagine, and other times he can be smaller than a speck. Even though some of his powers have weakened through Vindamar's spells over him, he's still a very powerful creature. If anyone can get you into Vindamar's castle, it's Gundar. Come, I'll tell you more on the way, but we must hurry if we are to meet up with him in three days."

A thick blanket of clouds covered the moon and made it very difficult to see as they traveled. Mela tried to keep Paige going at a steady pace, but Paige found it hard to keep up with her. At last Paige bent over, gasping for air.

"I'll see if we can stop here while you catch your breath," Mela said.

She sniffed the air then turned back to Paige. "I'm sorry, but we have to keep going. Something out there is following us—I'm not sure what or who it is. It'll be light soon, and there's a canyon not far from here. We can rest and have something—" Mela stopped speaking and looked around.

"What's wrong?" Paige whispered, trying to detect an enemy in the surrounding darkness.

"I'm not sure if there is anything wrong, but whatever it is, it's getting closer. We need to keep moving." She tugged at Paige, and they moved on. They didn't stop until the sun peeked over the mountain ridge.

"Look, Paige—see where the sun hits the peak of that mountain and makes it pink? That is where Gundar waits for our arrival."

Paige wiped the sweat from her brow. "Does this mean we made it?"

"That we did." Mela howled with delight. "Just beyond those large boulders is a canyon that will supply us with cover, water, and food. Princess, if you don't mind picking the black berries and green leaves over there, I'll see if I can find us some roots to eat. The roots will help us rest, and the berries and leaves will soothe the hunger pangs in our stomachs. There's a natural spring to quench our thirst once we get into the cave. I won't be long. If you need, anything just call me."

"I don't know, Mela. Are you sure those berries are okay for me to eat? The last time I ate berries, they almost killed me."

Mela went over to one of the bushes. "If you stick with these berries you'll be fine."

Paige picked and ate from the berries Mela indicated. She started to fill her pocket with some of the berries when she heard rustling in a nearby bush. Suddenly she heard a voice.

"And who do we have here?"

"Who said that?" she asked, turning around.

A serpent slithered out from under a bush. "One so young shouldn't be traveling alone."

"I'm not alone. Mela is with me."

"Mela?" the serpent asked. "I can't believe she left your side. She's slipping in her old age."

Paige backed away from the snake. "What do you want?"

"Mela didn't tell you about me? Aww, that's too bad. You see, I'm a friend of—"

"Ludwicka!" Mela yelled as she charged to Paige's aid.

She positioned herself between Paige and Ludwicka. "I had a feeling it was you." She growled, and the hackles on her back stood up.

"Now, Mela, is that any way to treat an old friend?"

"We're not friends, nor have we ever been friends!"

Ludwicka hissed as she coiled to strike. "Oh, I almost forgot. I have a message from Atwood."

"Atwood? What about Atwood?" she asked, taking another step toward Ludwicka.

"Atwood wanted me to tell you," Ludwicka screamed, lunging toward Mela, "that he's sorry that he couldn't protect your little darlings."

With a leap into the air, Mela eluded Ludwicka's strike. Mela and Ludwicka continued to fight as Paige tried several times to find a way to help with her magic staff.

Unsuccessful, she watched in horror as the dust rose and hisses and growls echoed throughout the canyon.

A dreadful yelp filled the dusty air, and then there was silence. When the dirt finally settled, Mela lay motionless, barely breathing.

"Mela!" Paige screamed and dashed over to where she lay. Paige dropped to her knees. Mela," she whispered as she held her in her arms.

Ludwicka slithered closer. "Mela…Mela, how charming." She hissed and coiled for another deadly strike. "Now it's your turn to join the others. It's too bad that I have to kill such a beauty." With that, Ludwicka sprang to sink her venomous teeth into Paige.

Out of nowhere, the dragon that had rescued Paige from the quicksand pit swooped down and took Ludwicka's strike then flew off.

Mela managed to lift her head high enough to catch Ludwicka between her strong jaws. She chomped down and killed Ludwicka before she closed her eyes, and then she took her last breath.

CHAPTER 19
ALONE

Paige didn't know what to do. She would hold Mela's body for a while, and then she would pick up her staff and demand Mela to wake up. When that didn't work, she tossed her staff to the ground and sat next to Mela. She wept as she stroked Mela's fur and asked her forgiveness for involving her, her pups, and Atwood.

The day passed in a haze, and afternoon was about to turn into evening when Paige looked up at the sky and saw buzzards circling overhead. "Get! Get out of here! Go on!" she shouted, waving her arms at the buzzards. She looked back down at the fallen wolf. "Don't worry, Mela. I won't let them get you."

She pounded the ground to loosen the dirt with her staff then used her hands to shovel it out. Even though her hands became raw and bloody, she never stopped until she had dug a hole large enough for Mela's body.

Next, she gathered ferns and leaves to line the empty grave and then laid Mela into her resting place. Paige cried as she covered her with the rest of the ferns she had gathered, then pushed the dirt over her with her hands.

Afterward, she carried enough large stones and rocks to cover the grave. She even managed to find a couple of sticks that she lashed together with the sleeves of her shirt, and made a small cross to prop at the head of Mela's grave.

She took off the necklace her father had made her and placed it on the cross. "It's not over," she whispered as beads of sweat and tears dripped onto the grave. Then she stood, raised her staff toward the sky, and shouted, "I'll find you, Vindamar, and when I do, you'll pay for what you've done! You'll pay for everyone you've hurt and taken away! You'll pay!"

She didn't rest after the burial. Outraged over Mela's death, she strode through the enveloping darkness. "I don't know how you will pay for what you have done, Vindamar, but you will pay!" she screamed into the night.

"I'll find a way to make sure your death isn't quick, and I'll make you squirm like the snake you are!"

Her hatred fostered the growing darkness in her mind, and her anger festered into rage as her skin became weathered and dry. As she pulled on her matted hair to untangle it, she clinched her teeth and muttered, "I'm going to torture you before I let the birds pick out your eyes. You will beg for mercy, and you will not have it."

Unaware that she was falling under Vindamar's curse, Paige welcomed the evil that took over her soul. Like so many others, she was now under the darkness of Vindamar's evil curse of hatred, and she wandered endlessly, trapped in Vindamar's Land of Indignation, alone and confused.

Without food or water, she was in danger of losing her life. Mumbling and weak, she dropped to her knees. "I can't do this anymore," she said quietly, and then she collapsed face down on the ground. "I'm hurt, worn out, and alone." She managed to raise her head enough to gaze at her staff where it lay. She stretched her arms and fingers out as far as she could and tried to pull herself closer to the staff, but she was too weak to reach it.

"Grandma, I can't feel you anymore. I thought you gave me the staff because it was part of you, so why do I feel so alone?" She lay motionless in her despair, but then thunder shook the ground, lightning lanced the sky, and small droplets of water fell. "Water," she whispered, and she managed to roll onto her back. She opened her mouth, and the droplets of rain moistened her dry tongue and blistered lips.

The rain continued while Paige envisioned herself back on the beach, meeting Noah for the first time. I wonder what he's doing? I wish he were here. He was so kind, even though I tried so hard to be hateful. He didn't know I couldn't have anyone around while I—Dad! I forgot about Dad! Too weak to walk, Paige rolled back onto her stomach. "I have to help Dad," she moaned as a flash of lightning forked across the sky.

The rain turned into hard pellets that slammed against her back. She gathered her strength and crawled over to retrieve her staff. She sipped water from a puddle before she stood. Still very weak, she stumbled, and as she fell, another flash of lightning lit up the area. There before her eyes was the cross and the necklace she had used to mark Mela's grave.

"No! I've gone in circles!" she screamed, and then she passed out; hitting her head on the rocks that covered Mela's grave.

CHAPTER 20

GUNDAR

Gundar knew something was terribly wrong when Mela didn't come. He asked around the forest to find out if anyone had heard from her. When word got back to him that a young girl who had been traveling with Mela was wandering alone in the Canyon of Gaithe, he set out immediately to find her.

"Who do we have here?" Gundar asked when he finally came upon her. She seemed to be regaining consciousness. *Something is not right. I feel Mela's presence, but where is she?* he thought.

Paige moaned and tried to open her eyes at the sound of his voice. Gundar leaned over her. "Hmm...I see there is dried blood on your forehead, and you carry the staff of Morwenna. Are you...?"

Paige opened her eyes and saw the huge, hairy spider that hovered over her. She tried to scream, but nothing came out, so she tried feebly to back away.

"It's okay. I'm Gundar, a friend of Mela's."

"Gundar?" she asked. "I should have known from Mela's description of you. Mela...." She started to cry.

Gundar became smaller so that he could draw closer to Paige. "It's okay. I'm here now."

"You don't understand. Ludwicka killed Mela. You should have seen the look on her face when Ludwicka told her she had killed her babies... and Atwood." Her sobs increased, and he realized the grave was Mela's, and that Paige must have buried her.

"I'm sorry to hear that. Mela was a dear friend to many. Look," he pleaded, "Mela will be missed, but right now I need to get you out of here before Vindamar's spies find you."

"Let him find me," she said fiercely. "Vindamar has to pay for what he's done."

"Sounds good, but right now you have a nasty bump on your head, and you're in no condition to fight anyone. If you can get on my back, I will carry you."

Paige became dizzy the moment she tried to stand. "I can't. Just leave me here."

"I'm not leaving you. There is another way I can get you to my home."

With his front legs, Gundar tapped out a message on the ground. It wasn't long before several creatures came to his aid. "Paige, these are some of my friends."

He pointed to a group of spiders, a Centaur, a Chimera, some Furies, and many other earthly and mythological creatures. "They're here to help me. The spiders will spin a web around you and the stretcher we'll prepare while the others help me keep watch. Don't worry. I'll get you out of this place and into the safety of my home."

Paige lay in silence as the creatures made their preparations, and fragments of her encounter with Mela replayed in her head: Gundar is one of the oldest and wisest warriors ever known. If anyone can get you into Vindamar's castle, it's Gundar… Gundar…Gundar….

CHAPTER 21

GUNDAR'S HOME

The spiders spun their webs over Paige and the small twigs placed around her by the woodland creatures. She drifted in and out of conscious while muskrats carried her on the stretcher, but when the procession made its way into the underground tunnels, she felt wide awake. She shivered against the dampness of the enclosed earth around her. I wonder if this is what it was like in the caverns of the great pyramids of Egypt? she thought. It probably has bottomless pits, filled with creatures ready to attack. She tried to hide under some of the webbing that held her onto the stretcher as thoughts of unexpected bats and crawling vipers ready to strike plagued her mind. She kept thinking of Ludwicka and Mela's battle; it would haunt her for the rest of her life.

Fireflies lit up the chambers they passed, giving her the opportunity to view the unique webbing that lined the walls and entrances. The light made her feel a little more secure; she would be able to see any enemies. Gundar, who was leading the way through the tunnels, stopped and then motioned for the muskrats to do the same.

"I see you're finally awake."

"Where am I?" Paige asked as she tried to sit up.

"We are underground in one of the many chambers of my home." Gundar replied.

Paige rubbed her forehead confused. She didn't know if she was dreaming or awake. "Underground! But it's lit up."

"I've asked the fireflies to come along so you wouldn't feel so disoriented. Why don't you close your eyes and rest? We can talk later." Gundar motioned for the muskrats to pick up the stretcher and continue on as Paige went back to sleep.

When Paige awoke she found herself in a well-lit room vented with fresh air by a hole in the earthen ceiling. She managed to get out of bed and stumbled over to a basin collecting water that trickled down a slippery ceramic wall. She dipped her hands into the refreshing water and took a few sips before she splashed it onto her face.

Feeling a bit more refreshed, she glanced around at her surroundings. There were no windows, but candles lit the room, and the bed she had been in was made from the earth's red clay covered in silk webbing. She went over to a small table and took an apple from a small bowl filled with fresh fruit and vegetables and started to devour the apple.

She took the coin out of her pocket and sat down on the bed. "It's only a matter of time before I find you, Vindamar," she whispered as she stuck the coin back into her pocket. She had just taken another bite of apple when someone knocked on the door.

"May I come in?" a soft voice asked.

Paige's mouth fell opened when she saw that a fairy had walked into the room. The fairy had long, fiery hair that she adorned with intertwining flowers: dewberry blossoms, silver bells, forget-me-nots, and star of Bethlehem. Her dress went from shades of blue and green to silver and gold, and her wings shimmered in the candlelight.

"Hi, I'm Nechama. Gundar asked me to look in on you and to bring you these clean clothes. Can I get you anything else?" she asked, placing the clothes on a chair next to the bed.

Paige managed to swallow her bite of apple. "Thanks for the clothes, but I have to go. How do I get out of here and to Vindamar's castle?"

"But Gundar brought you here so Vindamar wouldn't find you."

"Gundar should've left me out there. I want Vindamar to find me."

"I don't think so," Gundar said as he walked in. "You're my responsibility."

"Who said?" asked Paige.

Gundar left the room for a brief moment and returned with Paige's staff. "I found this next to you. I wonder who it belongs to."

She went over and retrieved her staff. "It's mine. So what?"

"Well, if it belongs to you, then you are my responsibility," he said as he motioned for Nechama to leave.

"I know Morwenna must have given you that staff, but the coin you hide in your pocket tells me the real secret as to who you are."

Paige felt annoyance surge up inside of her. "Since you know who I am, then I demand you take me to Vindamar."

"Demand! You don't have the right to make demands on me or anyone here." Angry, Gundar turned to leave but stopped. He did not face Paige as he continued to speak. "I'm sure your grandmother did not bring you up to be this way. You have much to learn before you are entitled to demand." He turned back and faced Paige. "You want to succeed, don't you?"

"Of course I do."

"Then don't be impatient. Your time will come soon enough." He paused at the door. Eat and rest. If you need anything, ask Nechama." He left the room, and Nechama came back in.

"Where were his manners?" Paige asked.

"Don't be quick to judge him," she replied. "You know, some have said Gundar may be Teutates or Odin in disguises. He has fought many battles and lost many friends because of Vindamar."

Nechama hesitated before she started to leave. "Is there anything I can get you before I leave?" she asked.

Paige shook her head, and the fairy left her to her thoughts.

CHAPTER 22

PREPARATIONS

It took several days for Paige to recover from her head injury and exposure to the heat. She continued to nag Gundar about Vindamar whenever he came to visit her, but being the warrior he was, Gundar felt it was too soon. He told Paige that her broken heart kept her a prisoner, and it made her unable to learn the skills needed to take on Vindamar.

He never gave up on her, and in time, with Gundar's guidance and kindness, Paige's heart softened, and the darkness inside her lifted. Her willingness to listen and learn grew, and she realized it wasn't just about her anymore, but the life around her.

During Paige's recovery, Gundar wasted no time teaching her the history of the Zandorians and the Andalarians. He told her that in AD 600, King Torin, a well-respected warlock, ruled over the land of Zandora, but it was a time when injustice and evil blanketed the land. He said that Merlin was saddened by a dream, and went to his friend King Torin to reveal his vision.

Merlin predicted that King Torin would have two sons: The first would use his powers to curse the land with droughts and hardships, and destroy all that was good by seeding confusion and hate in the minds of man; the second son would labor with his fellow man to bring fruit to barren lands. He would find ways to bring hope to the hearts that were lost and would bring mercy through forgiveness to those who asked. Merlin also explained how the older son would bring an end to the younger son's life.

King Torin wouldn't hear of it. Instead, he tried to bring reassurances to Merlin's fears about his firstborn, but as the years passed, he realized that Merlin's prophecy had become a reality, for no one was more ferocious and feared than Vindamar.

"Vindamar!" Paige exclaimed. "So you knew Vindamar."

"Yes. All the different tribes of the world came together and formed a legion to fight Vindamar, but nothing has worked. I and others have made a promise to Merlin that we would keep the legion between the different tribes, the woodland, and the humans strong and ready to stand behind the maiden who would bring justice, joy, and hope back to our land."

As Paige became stronger, Gundar continued his many stories, taught her the art of self-defense and the use of magical spells, and told her secrets meant only for her. Very late one evening, he stopped with his stories to draw in the sand. He drew the layout and the hidden passageways of Vindamar's castle.

Paige tried to hide her yawn from him, but she was too slow in covering her mouth.

"Oh my!" he said. "I didn't notice how late it is. I've taken up enough time with stories and drawings; it's time I stopped. We can continue this conversation tomorrow."

Paige protested. "I'm not tired. Please continue."

"You may not be tired, but I have a lot of other things that I must get done tonight. I'll tell you what, Paige—if I can complete what I need to do tonight, then tomorrow I'll show you my surprise. I might even explain the symbols on the staff you hold so dear."

"Do I have a choice?" she asked.

"Only if you want to hear what I have to say," he whispered as he closed the door to her room.

Paige went over and picked up her staff. *So tomorrow I'll learn your meaning.* She propped it back up against the chair before she went to bed.

Gundar worked throughout the night. He sent for reinforcements to go over every detail of how they would get Paige into Vindamar's castle, what they would do once she was inside, and how she would retrieve the dewdrop crystal. All night long, he went from one room to another and met with the different legions of the world to go over their strategies. In one such room, Gundar checked on the preparations for a coat he had requested. He wanted to know if it was complete so that he could add some final touches. Still busy, he didn't notice the time and didn't get back to his room before Paige woke up.

Eager to learn more, Paige ran to Gundar's room only to find it empty. Alarmed, she called out for him. When there was no response, she began to feel frantic.

"Here I am," he said, approaching her from behind.

She gasped as she turned toward him. "I thought something had happened to you."

"I'm fine," he said. "I was out rounding up help for our journey."

"Our journey?"

"Yes, our journey. You didn't think I would let you go alone, now did you?"

She was touched by his loyalty, and relieved that she wouldn't have to go alone. "Gundar, you have done so much."

"Not another word. You have many friends who want to help you get to Vindamar's castle. Come, I promised you a surprise." Gundar went out of one room and into another. Paige entered behind him and saw an unusual spider wearing a vest, busy at work.

"Who's that?" she asked.

"That's Aster. He designed your coat."

Paige gazed at Aster; his vest stirred a memory. "It can't be—your vest! It's the same vest a taxi driver was wearing when he picked me up at the airport."

"Is it now?" replied Aster as he turned to Gundar. "Paige's coat is ready."

"A coat? Why do I need a coat?" she asked.

"Mind you, it is not an ordinary coat," Gundar added.

"Come, let's go back to your room. We can talk on the way."

The two walked the short distance to her room. "This coat is meant to help you when you go inside Vindamar's castle. Once you put it on, you'll become invisible—but there are problems. It is extremely hot inside the castle. I'm not sure how long it will take you to get in and out of there, and you may become overheated and will have to take the coat off. If that happens, you won't be able to put it back on. Once off, it will dissolve into dust.

Paige stroked the coat in awe. "So it will make me invisible."

"Yes, but it's important that you understand that we can get you into the castle with no problem. The problem lies in how long it will take you to secure the dewdrop crystal. If it takes you too long, I'm not sure if you can withstand the heat."

"Don't worry, Gundar. I'll be fine."

"Do you remember what we went over?"

"Yes, I remember."

"Well, I'm going over it again."

Gundar took her over to a chair and sat her down. "First, no matter what, you're to leave the coat on until you're out of the castle, even if you get overheated. Second—" Gundar went over to a table and took a scarf from one of the drawers and handed it to Paige. "Once you're in the castle and you've secured the dewdrop crystal, you are to toss this scarf out the closest window. There will be someone at each wall ready to retrieve it. Whoever retrieves this scarf will pass the message on to me that you have the crystal and you're on the way back to the door by which you entered. If anything goes wrong, and Vindamar discovers you're there, I'll have the troops advance at the front of the castle to distract Vindamar while I get you out with the crystal. Do you understand?"

"Yes, Gundar."

"Excellent. Now just one more question: are you ready for the challenge?"

Gundar noticed a fire in Paige's eyes and strength in her voice that had never been there before.

"Vindamar's rule over this land has gone on too long. He will soon know that the time has come for the legend of Zandora to be fulfilled."

CHAPTER 23

LAST NIGHT AS PAIGE

After a few days of traveling through the murky forest of Drusus, they finally arrived at the river's edge near Vindamar's castle. Paige, Gundar, and his army stopped just inside the forest. Paige was amazed to see more troops already in place; he hadn't told her there would be troops set up days before their arrival. He had also arranged an area of rest and protection for her.

"We'll wait here," Gundar said. "Most of Vindamar's spies should be back inside the castle by evening. We can get closer then."

He turned to Paige. "I need you to rest."

Paige glared at Gundar. "I appreciate your concern, but I want you to stop treating me like I'm a child. I'm not, and I'm not leaving you."

"You're right. You're not a child. Sorry."

Gundar bowed as he motioned for a couple of Faun guards to escort her. "I would appreciate it, my princess, if you would go with these guards. You may not be tired, but you need to be out of this heat and get something to eat. You will find the fresh berries and cool water quite refreshing. And if by chance you find the need to rest, there is a bed available. I promise you, Paige, you won't miss a thing. I will join you later, and we can go over everything." She grinned at him. "I'll go because you asked me, not because I want to or need to." Then she went with the guards.

When she walked into her quarters hidden by Gaea, her eyes widened. Like her room at Gundar's, it had all of the conveniences of home, right down to a jar of wild flowers on a small table.

"Excuse me, my princess. May I come in?" a young female badger asked.

"Gundar asked me to bring you something to eat and drink."

"Please, do come in." Paige smiled when the young badger placed a bowl of fresh berries and a cup of cool water on the table. "Thank you. I am a little hungry and thirsty."

"If there is anything else I can get you, my princess, I'll be just outside the door." The young badger bowed, and then turned to leave.

"There is one thing," she said before the badger could leave.

"Yes, my princess?"

"Please call me Paige, and there is more than I can eat. Would you please join me?" She pulled another chair up to the table. "You never gave me your name?"

"I'm Elle. I'll stay and join you in conversation, but I have already eaten more than I should have. Thank you for the offer."

Paige ate and drank while Elle told silly stories about her family and the things she once did to tease her siblings. It wasn't long before Paige herself started to tell Elle some of her own funny family stories. The two of them laughed so loudly that the guards outside peeked in to see what was going on. For the first time on her journey, Paige was able to relax and be seventeen again.

About halfway into the meal, Paige stopped laughing, put her elbows onto the table, and rested her forehead in her hands.

"Are you feeling all right?" Elle asked, then called out for help.

"I'm not sure. I feel a little woozy and the roooom…." Paige slurred the words. She stood up to go toward the bed, but she fell back onto the chair just as Harrison, a Faun, entered the room.

"I'll help you," he said. He lifted Paige and gently laid her down on the bed.

"I don't know what happened. One minute we were laughing, and the next minute she was dizzy!" the young badger cried, staring at Paige in concern.

"Harrison looked at Elle, "It's okay, Gundar put a sleeping spell on her water. He wanted to make sure the princess rested before she went into battle."

CHAPTER 24

PLANS TO ENTER VINDAMAR'S CASTLE

Gundar walked in just as Elle placed a blanket over Paige. "I see our princess is already asleep." He went over to Paige and whispered into her ear, "Forgive me, Princess, but I took an oath to watch over you and keep you safe. You need to rest; it's going to be a long night."

Before he left, he placed Harrison to stand guard outside Paige's quarters, then gave orders that no one was to disturb her. He also told him, "If Paige awakens before my return, make sure she stays put. Tell her I will come for her when it is time. I need to prepare for our princess's entry into the castle. I trust you will inform me when she is awake."

"Yes, sir."

"Good." Gundar left the guard to his duties. He met with the woodland creatures first and went over every detail of Vindamar's castle and the grounds. Afterward, he gathered his troops to prepare them for what was about to happen. He repeatedly stressed how important it was that until the princess secured the dewdrop crystal no one was to enter the castle. He reminded them that if they did, they would put not only their princess at risk, but also the world.

As night approached, Gundar and his army continuously monitored the comings and goings at the castle. Gundar paced as he waited to hear from an owl that pretended to work for Vindamar.

The owl's job was to patrol the outside of the castle at night and let Gundar know when all of Vindamar's spies were inside. Once Gundar received word that the spies had retreated inside the castle walls, he would advance his troops to the castle's front and side walls, while he and Paige retreated to a secret back entrance.

Paige slept as Gundar finalized the plans to get her inside the castle. It wasn't until nightfall that she opened her eyes and looked around. What happened? she thought, as she sat up still feeling a little woozy.

"Gundar!" She jumped out of bed, grabbed her staff and rushed outside to find Gundar. "Out of my way," she demanded, trying to push Harrison aside with her staff.

"I'm sorry," said Harrison, "but you can't leave. Gundar asked me to keep you here until he came for you."

Paige was furious. "Are you forgetting who you're speaking to? Either get out of my way or come with me—I don't care—but I'm leaving."

"As you wish." Harrison bowed. "I'll take you to Gundar." He took her directly to Gundar's tent where they were still going over last-minute details.

"I'm sorry, Gundar, but she insisted."

"It's okay," Gundar said and nodded for the others to leave him with Paige.

"Before you say anything let's go outside. I thought you weren't tired." He smiled, keeping a watchful eye over the campsite. Silence fell over them, and neither looked at the other as they stared out over the burned-out meadow ahead.

Fuming, Paige couldn't hold her silence any longer. "You made me sleep somehow, didn't you? I'm so angry at you!"

"Rightly so, my princess." He tapped his front leg on the ground a few times.

"So…how do you feel?" he asked. He still didn't look at her.

"Rested." Paige looked at Gundar and started to laugh in spite of herself. She had to admit, she did feel more rested for her mission tonight than if she had stayed awake all day.

"Thanks, Gundar."

He met her gaze. "You're welcome. Now that all is forgiven and you're rested, do you think you're ready to hear what the symbols mean on your staff? This may take a while, so you may want to sit down."

Excited to hear the story, Paige gave her staff to Gundar. He pointed at the different symbols as he explained them.

"The circles here represent the outer universe: the sun, moon, and stars. A long time ago, the outer universe brought gifts to the Earth.

Their gift of light, which is represented by these lines here, brought balance to Earth's climate. The moon controlled the tides of the oceans and much more. See here?"

He pointed to the symbols that looked like humans and animals interacting with one another. "You will see how the creatures and humans speak to each other? Believe it or not, all creatures—humans, animals, and magical creatures that roamed this land—spoke and listened to each other like you and I do. We all understood how we brought balance to each other, just like the outer universe understood and balanced with the inner. We all understood that a mighty creator made everything with a purpose. This way we all would have to work together."

Before he could finish, an owl approached him with a message, then took a place alongside the other creatures that had gathered to help Gundar. Gundar turned toward Paige and bowed.

"Your Highness, I will have to continue this another day, but it's time to put our plan in motion." Gundar handed Paige her staff, then gathered the troops and gave them the command to advance. Paige nervously took in a few deep breaths as she pulled her hair back, shrugged her shoulders, and paced as she waited for Gundar to give the word that they were on their way to the castle.

While the troops advanced, Gundar waved in the mighty Piasa bird, feared and known as evil by humans. The large creature had the face of a man, but with red eyes, and it had deer's antlers and a tiger's beard. Its body was covered in red, black, and green scales, and its tail was so long that it could circle its own body twice. The Piasa lowered its enormous body close to the ground so Gundar and Paige could climb onto its back. Once its tail was wrapped securely around them, it flew them toward the back of the castle.

The castle's rear wall had only one ledge available to land on, but the ledge was too small for the Piasa, so Gundar instructed it to drop them off on the ground.

Paige looked at the webbing that Gundar had his friends spin days earlier for her use. "Nice work!" she said as she tugged on the web.

Gundar had some spiders ready to help him lash Paige's staff onto her back.

"Now remember; your staff is only a backup in case your coat becomes damaged, so do not try to unlash it unless you really need it." Once they were done he turned her around to face him.

"Before you go up that wall, I want to remind you, we can't get into the castle to help you until you have secured the crystal, and remember Batty. He will show you the way to the crystal. Got it?"

"Yes, Gundar."

"Let's see. Have I forgotten anything?" he asked, checking her over to make sure she had everything.

"Would you stop worrying? I'll be fine. You taught me well."

Without a word, Gundar bowed down to Paige, and then they just stared at each other.

"Gundar, I need to get up that wall before it's daylight."

Gundar took her hand. "Many centuries ago, I was one of a very few who took an oath alongside Merlin, King Torin, and your grandmother to protect you. Before you go into the castle, I want you to know the coat I gave you is like the staff you carry. I will be with you in spirit, as is Morwenna. By the time I and my troops enter the castle, the universe will know that the maiden of Zandora was here and that you, Autumn Jorah Mist, have fulfilled your destiny."

Paige was touched by his words. "Oh, Gundar! You never called me that before. I wouldn't be here if it hadn't been for you, Grandma, Mela, Atwood, and all the other creatures that are here to help me fight Vindamar. Together we will bring him down. It will be a victory for all of us."

She kissed Gundar on his head then reached into her pocket and took out the coin and placed it in his hand.

"If by chance Vindamar finds me, I don't want him to get this coin. Keep it safe. You can give it back to me when we meet again." She turned to climb up the wall.

"Wait!" he whispered. "You forgot to put on your coat!"

As he helped her into the coat, he asked nervously, "Did I mention that once you take the coat off it loses its powers?"

"Yes, Gundar. Don't worry, I've remembered everything you told me. I'm to keep this coat on until I'm out of the castle, and if by chance my coat rips, then I have my staff as a backup."

She turned toward the wall and took hold of the webbing. She pulled in a deep breath, and then started the long climb up the steep castle wall.

CHAPTER 25

BATTY

Paige scaled the castle's north wall, only to stop short of pulling herself up onto the ledge—she heard voices coming from inside.

I thought Gundar said no one uses this entrance. She stayed still and listened to the conversation that went on inside.

"Did you hear that?" Batty asked the other bats that hung upside down near the wall opening.

"Hear what?" another asked.

"Stop being so paranoid, Batty," said Catigern. "Nothing is out there."

"Oh no, Batty, maybe it's your mother," another joked as he flew around Batty.

Paige carefully pulled herself onto the ledge, then leaned against the inside wall.

"There it is again!" Batty said. "I think someone is out there. Maybe someone should go out and look."

Catigern finally gave in. "I'll tell you what, Batty. If you stop being so jumpy, I'll go out there and check things out."

The other bats laughed when Catigern gave into Batty's complaints.

"Okay, guys," Catigern said, interrupting their laughter. "It's the only way any of us will get any peace and quiet around here. Come on; let's go check things out. Not you, Batty," he added as Batty tried to join them. "You stay here. I wouldn't want the boogieman to get you." He laughed as he waved for the rest of the bats to follow.

Paige stayed still as all the bats left the castle—all but one.

"Who's there?" Batty asked, sniffing around where she stood. "I know someone is here. I'm Batty; if you have a message from Gundar, tell me before the others come back. If not then you'd better go. You don't have much time."

"You're Gundar's friend?" Paige asked, and Batty focused his eyes in the direction of her voice. "He said you would show me the secret room where Vindamar keeps the dewdrop crystal."

"I'll be happy to show you, but surely Gundar has told you that the room has a spell on it. No one has ever entered that room without Vindamar's knowledge, and it's not a pretty ending when he finds an intruder."

"Don't worry; let me handle it. I just need to know how to get to the room."

Batty pointed with his wing to a nearby corridor. "Follow this corridor. There will be a door on the left; it will take you to a room near the dewdrop crystal. I'll come to you once the others return and take their places for the evening. Word is out that the maiden is on her way, and that Gundar has an army to retrieve the dewdrop crystal. Vindamar also has the black agate."

"So Grandma was right. He does have the black agate. Where does he keep it?" Paige asked.

"He wears it around his neck. Didn't Gundar get my message? I sent word to him not long ago that Vindamar has the black agate and the dewdrop crystal. You must leave now. Catigern and the others are coming. Just follow the cobblestones to the first door on your left. Go quickly."

Without a second to waste, Paige left down the corridor while Batty kept the other bats distracted with his babbling.

CHAPTER 26

UNEXPECTED GUEST

Paige ran her fingers along the surface of the wall as if she were reading a book in Braille. It took a while before she could find the door, for the corridor was dark and the cobblestone path made it difficult to walk.

First door to the left...this must be it. She opened the door, and tried to hurry inside, but her staff got caught up on the L-shaped door handle. Once she was able to get her staff free she closed the door behind her.

Oh great my coat is torn. She tried to untie the lashing that held her staff to her back, but the more she struggled, the more her movements unraveled her coat. Frustrated, she ripped off what was left of her coat then looked around the room for a good place to hide her staff.

The only light came from the moon's rays through a tiny window, but it was enough for Paige to see a large canopy bed. One wall was covered in hand-carved panels of black walnut depicting images of flowers, trees, and fairies; it reminded her of her grandmother's living room. Moss lined the adjoining limestone walls.

On top of the dresser, a brush and comb set was neatly arranged on a mirror. An untouched bottle of perfume sat next to a music box shaped like a birdcage. Inside the birdcage was a miniature nightingale, looking as if it wanted to sing to the world. It would be nice if I could hear what you sound like.

Just as she picked up the music box to get a better look she heard a voice from across the hall. She tiptoed to the door and cracked it open. To her astonishment, she saw Noah across the corridor. He appeared to be talking to himself.

"Noah?" she gasped as she ran to him.

Noah looked stunned. "Paige? How did you get here? Were you kidnapped, too?"

"Kidnapped? No. Why were you kidnapped?"

"This guy asked me about a black agate. When I didn't tell him anything, he brought me here, saying that he knew I had it. What's going on, Paige? What's so important about that black agate?"

"Oh, I'm so sorry, Noah. The last thing I wanted was to get anyone mixed up in my troubles. That's why I was so mean to you at the beach."

"What kind of trouble are you in?"

She looked down at the floor. "All I can say is it's a long and weird story."

He took her hands. "Look, Paige, I'm already involved. It can't get any stranger than this. Come and have a seat."

"I guess you're right. What I'm about to tell you may seem impossible, but it's true." Paige sat with Noah and told him that she needed the black agate to break the spell Vindamar had over her father and the people of Zandora. She explained how the stone he had given herwas cursed and why she needed to get the dewdrop crystal back to its rightful place.

She told him that Atwood, Mela, and her pups had given up their lives to help her, and that a dragon came out of nowhere and saved her from death twice. "I'm sorry, Noah. Can you ever forgive me?" she asked as she stood up.

"I should've been honest with you from the beginning. If I had, you wouldn't be here. I have to get you out of here. This is not your fight; it's mine."

Noah took her in his arms and gave her a long hug. "Don't be silly. With you in my arms, it's worth being kidnapped."

"And what do we have here?" a man asked as he walked in on Paige and Noah.

"Nothing, Uncle." Noah's voice squeaked as he pulled away from Paige. "I thought it would be funny to listen to a foolish girl talk. A pleasure, Paige." He turned and walked out of the room, leaving Paige alone with Vindamar.

CHAPTER 27
CAPTURE OF THE MAIDEN

Vindamar stared at Paige as she stood there, stunned. "How easy you make it for me, Paige. I thought it would be much harder."

"Harder—harder for what? Judging by your appearance, you must be the great Vindamar the sorcerer, who stole the black agate I see around your neck."

"Ah yes, the black agate." Vindamar laughed. "You see, my dear, I've had it all along. When my nephew told me you were looking for it, I gave him a cursed stone to give to you.

Though he didn't know that stone was cursed and should've turned you into Undines when you were near water. The thing I couldn't figure out when I heard you speaking with my Nephew was how you were able to make it here and how you knew enough to toss it into the river before the spell took hold of you. Then it came to me—you're the granddaughter of Morwenna. I knew you would come to me. I just had to wait patiently. It isn't one of my strong points, I admit."

"Oh, I don't know," Paige said, seeing his smirk. "From what I've heard, you've waited centuries for this day."

"It doesn't matter." He laughed again. "Oh how joyous.

What a brilliant plan. Not only do I have the black agate and the dewdrop crystal, but now I also have Autumn Mist, the granddaughter of Morwenna. I've prepared a room fit for you, dear princess." He raised his hands high into the air. "How delightful. If only my father and brother could see me now.

So, Autumn Mist—or do you prefer Paige? What would you do for this black agate?" He dangled it in front of her, and then started a chant. "Ouy era reverof enim dna on eno llahs tsetorp."

With those words, Paige fell under his spell. Unable to move, she stood there as he stroked her long, wavy hair, then sniffed the back of her neck. "Oh, my beautiful Autumn Mist, so we meet again. I know you can hear me," he whispered into her ear.

"You wouldn't remember me, but I met you when you were just a baby. Your father and I were friends at one time. I should have known you were the maiden. It was foretold that my dead brother had made plans for his son Noah to marry you. I can't let that happen."

He became agitated as he put his hands on her shoulders. "My father thought he could give my throne away to my brother, and my brother thought by getting rid of the coin, his son would be king, but look where it got him. I will be the one to marry you. I will be king.

"My darling," he said, calming down again, "you should know I'm the one who rules this universe—no one else. Once we're married, no one can stop me. Not only will I have my place on the throne, but all will bow down to me. Vindamar! Everyone and everything will do as I say or die."

He laughed as he took her by the hand and led her into another room. "Come. I've prepared a room for you. It's the same room you were in earlier. You will find a wedding dress laid out on the bed, and next to it is a veil. A beautiful bride you shall be."

As Vindamar walked Paige to the room he had prepared, he continued to taunt her. "Knowing you can only do as I say brings joy to my heart. You shall now get ready to marry me."

Paige nodded in compliance and went over to a white satin-and-lace wedding dress adorned with pearls, beads, and sequins. Next to it was a veil as long as her dress, crowned with wildflowers. Vindamar left the room and closed the heavy door behind him, then called out to his bat servant. "Catigern, make sure no one enters this room; my bride is getting ready for our wedding. If you need me, I'll be in the dungeon. There is much to be done."

CHAPTER 28

THE DECEPTION

As Paige got ready for her wedding, Batty went to Noah's room. "Noah! Noah!"

"What do you want, Batty?"

"Your uncle plans to marry Paige! Tonight!"

Stunned, Noah turned around to face Batty. "What did you say?"

"Vindamar is in the dungeon right now, getting things ready so he can marry Paige."

"You must be mistaken, Batty."

"No, I'm not. You need to get down there before something terrible happens."

"Okay, I'll talk to my uncle to see what's going on, but I think you're blowing this out of proportion."

He walked to the dungeon and pushed open the huge doors. His uncle looked busy mixing up his usual potions, but there was a large assortment of flowers, ribbons, and candles all around the room. That was very unusual. He entered the dungeon. "Uncle, what are you doing down here? It looks like you're getting ready for a wedding. Who's getting married?"

Vindamar turned to Noah. "If you must know, Paige has agreed to marry me."

Batty was right. "What? This doesn't make sense," he spluttered. "Why would Paige marry you when she doesn't even know you?"

Vindamar stopped mixing. "You're right, of course. We don't know each other, but the fact is that Paige's father betrothed her to me at birth. She is of age, and it's time she and I married."

"Betrothed? You never said anything about a betrothal." Noah tried to keep his voice calm. "How does she feel about this?"

Vindamar looked him right in the eye. "She has agreed to marry me; you can ask her yourself. She is getting ready as we speak."

He approached Noah and put his hand on his right shoulder. "I know this comes as a surprise, but Paige knew her destiny long before she came to the castle. She knew the one who held the black agate was to be her husband. She noticed the black agate around my neck and knew I was her betrothed. This wasn't my idea; it is the law of her world and ours. It was the two worlds that bound Paige's destiny to mine."

Noah backed away from him and began to pace back and forth. "Then why did you want me to give her the black agate? Why didn't you just do it yourself?"

Vindamar could see that Noah had trouble believing his story; he had to come up with something fast.

"Well, since you asked, this stone is cursed. If I had given you the black agate around my neck it would have been certain death for you. I didn't want that to happen, so I created another black agate. I hoped that by creating another one, Paige would think you were the one bound to her. Unfortunately, it didn't work out that way. When she saw the black agate around my neck, she instantly knew I was her betrothed. She knew it was the one that her father had cut. Then she reminded me that we were bound by law, and we must do what we are bound by. Anything less would result in disaster. Paige is the one who insisted that we marry tonight, so the two worlds could find peace and harmony."

"None of this makes any sense."

"Noah, Paige deserves to be happy. She has seen and felt so much pain in the last few weeks. She told me about how she was looking for the person who had the black agate, and how it brought her on a long journey of mishaps. I'm not going to be the one to stand in her way to happiness."

"Okay, Uncle, if this is what Paige wants."

Vindamar hid his smirk. "It's not what I would have chosen for her, but this wedding must take place. I have everything prepared, but there is something you could do for her. Since no one is here to give her away, maybe you could do that."

"I don't know…"

"Of course you can. All you need to do is walk her down the aisle, and when she gets to the front of the altar, place her hand in mine; give her the chalice to drink from, and say, 'Paige, drink of the chalice, for I give your hand in marriage to Vindamar, and with this you and Vindamar shall be bound forever.'"

"Paige really wants me to do this?" "Ask her!"

Noah looked him in the eyes. "This seems so weird, Uncle. I can't believe this is what she wants, but if it's true, then I'll do it."

Vindamar patted him on the back. "This is what Paige and I want more than anything. You don't know how happy this will makes us. Now go and get ready—things should be in place within the hour. You will see for yourself; this wedding was meant to be."

CHAPTER 29

NOAH LEARNS THE TRUTH

Noah left his uncle to the wedding preparations and went back to his room. He found Batty waiting for him. As soon as he shut the door, Batty started questioning him. "Did you speak to Vindamar? What did he say? You're not going to let this marriage happen, are you?"

Batty saw darkness in Noah's eyes that had never been there before, and he heard the anger in his voice when he spoke. "Paige has made her decision. She's getting ready to marry my uncle—she can't wait to marry him. There's nothing I can do."

"That's not true, Noah. He put a spell on her—I saw him do it. Noah, listen to me," he insisted when it looked like Noah was tuning him out.

"There are things you don't know or understand about your uncle. I promised your father before he died that I would take care of you and protect you. I feared for your life, so I never told you about Vindamar and what he did to your father."

Noah grabbed Batty. "What about my father?"

"What I'm about to tell you I kept from you because I didn't want Vindamar to hold you captive, but if this wedding takes place, you will lose more than Paige."

"What are you trying to tell me, Batty?"

"I don't have time to tell you everything so here's the short version: Even before you were born, Merlin told King Torin—your grandfather— that one day he would have a grandson who would be king—not your father or your uncle. This weighed heavy on his heart; he could not understand why neither of his sons would be king, but as the years went by, he began to understand Merlin's predictions. It became clear that the only thing in Vindamar's heart was evil."

"But you said my father was a good man. Why didn't he become king?"

"Just hear me out, Noah. Your grandfather sent for Merlin. He wanted Merlin to know that he was going to give your father the gold coin. The problem came when he didn't wait for Merlin to arrive. His health was failing, and he didn't want to take any chances on Vindamar becoming king. He gathered only his closest kinsmen, your father, and Morwenna—who happens to be Paige's grandmother—into his chambers for a secret meeting."

"Wait…you're telling me Paige's grandmother was there?" Noah asked.

"Yes. In this meeting, King Torin explained Merlin's prophecy, and gave your father the gold coin to the throne. Word made it to Vindamar that your father would inherit the throne. He confronted your father after killing your grandfather and demanded that he tell him where the coin was. When that didn't work, he had your mother brought to him.

While he tortured your father in front of your mother, your father pleaded with your mother to say nothing. They both knew Vindamar would kill them after he had the coin, and the only way to save you was to keep their silence and make sure he did not find the coin. Vindamar killed your parents."

"Stop!" Noah pleaded. "I don't want to hear any more."

"I'm sorry, Noah, but you need to hear this. There are only three of us left who know what happened to the coin. Your father gave it to Morwenna for safekeeping. The agreement was to give Paige the coin when she was old enough to understand her destiny and old enough to marry you. Without that coin, Vindamar can't rule.

He knew the legend of Zandora—the maiden who will one day come and destroy him. He knew what he had to do to get the throne: First, he had to weaken the powers Paige's people had over him by getting the black agate and the dewdrop crystal. As soon as he acquired those, he was able to weaken the Zandorians. Now he has just one last obstacle to the throne—the gold coin.

"This is where you come in, Noah. Vindamar needs you to relinquish Paige as your bride, and to do that you have to give him her hand in marriage and pass the chalice of poison he has prepared for her to drink.

This poisoned potion will break the vows that were made between the inhabitants of Zandora and Andalar. All the powers you and Paige have will transfer to Vindamar. Under the laws of Zandora and Andalar, he will be granted the throne. "Vindamar killed your mother, father, and grandfather. The only reason you're still alive is because he needs you to relinquish your betrothal to Paige. Once she drinks from the chalice, Vindamar will have you killed."

Noah paced the room; his head felt full of truths he couldn't have imagined. "My uncle has made a fool out of me. This explains why my heart knew when she was in trouble. She was betrothed to me. I do know; I'll die before I ever give Paige to him. What am I going to do, Batty? He will kill Paige if I don't do something, and soon. I can't just go in there and kill him. His powers are stronger than mine."

"Noah, you have friends who are ready to fight alongside you, but for their safety and yours, I can't tell you who they are. For now, your job is to keep Vindamar from suspecting that you know the truth; don't let your anger interfere with your judgment. Your heart and mind are like your father's— you will know what to do when the time is right. You must go now, and get ready for a wedding."

CHAPTER 30

RETURN OF THE DRAGON

Down in the dungeon, Vindamar placed candles on each side of the red carpet that stretched from the back entrance to the front altar, creating an aisle for Paige to walk. A soft amber glow lit the aisle, and the aroma of lilies and orchids filled the once-stale air. As a final touch, ivy and colorful ribbons dangled from the ceiling. Vindamar wanted the preparations to seem flawless to give Noah the illusion that all was ideal between him and Paige. He didn't want anything to go wrong in the final stages of becoming king and taking over the world.

"I was just about to summon you," Vindamar told Catigern as he flew in.

Catigern laughed as he looked around. "Look at this place! And you—fixed up fancy and all. When did you turn all romantic and mushy?"

Vindamar only snarled. "Is she ready?" He turned to look in the mirror. He spat on his hands and rubbed them together, and then he ran his fingers though his hair. I hate having to look like a happy groom. It's not me. Let's get this over with!"

"As requested, your bride waits outside the doors." Vindamar turned away from the mirror.

"Where is that boy when I need him?"

"I passed his room on the way here," Catigern replied. "He should be here any minute."

"Not soon enough," Vindamar grumbled. "Once Noah gets here, I want you to immediately have him walk Paige to me. I'll be waiting at the altar."

100

He paced, agitated, and then he fixed his attention on the massive doors Paige stood behind. "Catigern!" he yelled.

"I'm right here sir."

He crossed his arms in front of his chest. "Tell me, what does she look like? Does her innocence shine through?"

"Well if you must know, sir, she is—"

"No, no, no, don't tell me. I want to be surprised. I'm thinking how fun it will be to take her as my bride before I destroy her." He clenched his hands together and turned to the closed doors.

"On second thought, we shouldn't leave her waiting outside. Open the doors so my bride may enter." On Vindamar's command, two warthogs turned the enormous wheel that opened the huge redwood doors. Vindamar, like any groom in anticipation, rubbed his hands together as he waited for his bride to enter.

Catigern and the other bats escorted Paige through the open doors, and stopped when Vindamar raised his hands and motioned for the doors to close again. Catigern kept Paige next to the redwood doors inside the dungeon, where they were to wait for Noah.

Vindamar's cold heart pounded when his eyes focused on Paige. "Your purity overwhelms me, my Autumn Mist. Never have I seen such beauty and innocence."

He moaned as he stepped off the altar steps. Suddenly, even though Noah hadn't arrived, Vindamar's voice rang out, "Start the music, and bring me my bride! She shall wait next to me."

As the music played, Paige walked gracefully down the candlelit aisle toward Vindamar. Her long veil and white dress covered the red carpet in the center of the aisle. Hypnotized by her beauty, no one noticed that the dragon lurking on the dark balcony above was now descending toward Vindamar.

"Watch out, Vindamar!" a bat yelled out. Catigern stopped Paige and then rushed to Vindamar's aid.

Before Vindamar could duck, the dragon grabbed the black agate from around his neck and dropped it at Paige's feet. Furious, Vindamar raised his hands toward the dragon and shouted, "Odum noar vixtiean." Bolts of lightning flashed from his hands and into the air. The lightning bolts just missed the dragon and bounced off the walls. Vindamar and the dragon continued to fight when others joined in.

Batty called in some of his bat friends and swooped down to picked up the black agate. He dropped it on Paige's bridal bouquet, but still in a trance, she was unable to take it.

Catigern saw what Batty tried to do and raced toward the agate as it dropped out of the flowers. Just as Catigern swooped to get the agate, another bat rammed into Catigern's side, sending Catigern to the ground. Batty picked up the agate and flew back to Paige. This time, he was able to place it securely in her hand.

The fighting continued between Catigern, Batty, and his friends while Vindamar yelled out spells that brought forth lightning bolts. One such bolt struck the dragon's wing and brought the dragon down. Vindamar swaggered to the fallen dragon, and then he raised his hand to strike the final blow.

"Vindamar!" Paige screamed out.

Vindamar stopped and turned toward Paige while the wounded dragon escaped into the darkness of the dungeon's balcony.

CHAPTER 31
MAKING A DECISION

The fighting ceased when everyone saw that Paige held the black agate.

"Vindamar!" she shouted. "I'm no longer under your spell. I hold the black agate."

All eyes went to Vindamar, for all knew Vindamar needed the black agate to keep his powers over Paige.

"Let's talk about this, Paige," he said as he slowly walked her way. "You said you wanted the black agate, and now you've got it."

"Stop right there. I have the black agate, and I demand that you restore its original red color, and I want the dewdrop crystal so it can be returned to its rightful place."

Vindamar took another step toward her. He glared at her as he quickly came up with a plan. "If you give me the black agate, I promise to release the dewdrop crystal to you. However, there is still the question of your father."

"What about my father?" she demanded.

"If you want me to take the spell off of him and return the dewdrop crystal, you will have to marry me first. Then and only then will I take the spell off your father. It will be my wedding gift to you."

He continued to take slow, small steps toward her. "My dear, all I ever wanted was you. I took your father, the black agate, and the dewdrop crystal because I knew you would do anything to get them back. I'm willing to give it all back for your hand in marriage."

Paige thought quickly. "I'll tell you what, Vindamar. I'll marry you as soon as you bring me the dewdrop crystal and return my father. I don't trust you."

The doors opened as Paige spoke, and Noah entered the dungeon. He looked around, confused—had there been a battle?—and then went to Vindamar's side.

"I thought you said she wanted to marry you," he whispered.

"This is no time for explanations," Vindamar said quietly. "Paige wants an early wedding gift. I need you to get the dewdrop crystal and pretend that you are taking it to her. Once you are close enough, grab the black agate from her and bring it to me. Understand?"

"Fine," Noah replied, and then he hurried out of the dungeon.

"Paige, I've instructed Noah to bring the dewdrop crystal back here. This will show you that I'm willing to keep our agreement." He could barely contain his victorious smirk.

Batty's reinforcements kept Catigern and his friends from following Batty as he followed Noah out of the dungeon. "You're not going to give Vindamar the crystal, are you?"

"No, Batty. Paige will have her crystal. If you have any friends to help out, now is the time to send for them. Let them know the Maiden of Zandora has arrived."

Batty went straight to Gundar, who waited just outside the castle gates.

Noah retrieved the crystal he had hidden in the east tower of the castle and returned to the dungeon, and Vindamar motioned for him to take it to Paige. With his back to Vindamar, Noah could gaze openly at Paige as he approached her. He never took his eyes from hers, and it gave him courage for what he felt he had to do.

When she reached out for the crystal, he placed it into the palms of her hands. Before she could move away, he gently brought her hands to his lips, and kissed them. Once the crystal was secured in her hands, he let them go and immediately lunged himself at her, driving the crystal deep into the left side of his chest, piercing his heart.

"No!" Paige screamed as she reached out to catch him. He was too heavy for her to hold onto. He hit the stone floor with a thud, and the black agate that Paige held now rested in his hand.

CHAPTER 32
THE BATTLE

Paige sobbed uncontrollably. "Noah!" she cried, kneeling on the floor trying to raise him up into her arms.

"Foolish child, see what happens when you try to fight me?" Vindamar laughed as he walked slowly toward Paige.

She ignored his taunts; all she could think of right now was Noah. "I'm so sorry, Noah. This wasn't supposed to happen." She tried to take his hand and noticed that the black agate he held was turning red. "Noah, you broke the spell with your blood," she whispered in his ear.

"See what you have done, Autumn Mist? If you had only listened to me, Noah would still be alive, and your father wouldn't be under my spell. Now I'm afraid I'll have to take care of your grandmother, too. I have this terrible vision in my head on how I will deal with her before I kill her." Vindamar grinned.

"You leave my grandmother out of this. It's me you want, not her," Paige screamed.

"Everyone you have ever loved will either die or fall under my control; I will do with them as I please." Vindamar's voice echoed throughout the dungeon; it sounded more menacing than ever.

Paige grabbed the agate out of Noah's hand and clenched it tightly as she stood up. "I didn't do this; you did!" she yelled, glaring into Vindamar's eyes. "You did this, and you're going to pay!"

The sound of horns and drums began to rise above the commotion inside the dungeon. "Do you hear that, Vindamar? Outside these castle walls are the strongest creatures from all corners of the world. They come with their weapons and bravery. Together they announce their arrival. Listen to their horns and the beat of their drums, Vindamar. Listen how they shout out their victory over you."

Hoping to gain control over Vindamar, Paige held up the agate, and started to chant. "Eb enog ot eht tip fo lleh morf erehw uoy emac." She kept up the chant as she stalked toward Vindamar. "Eb enog ot eht tip fo lleh morf erehw uoy emac."

Vindamar wasn't threatened. "Go ahead and chant all you want," he said with a smirk. "But as you can see, it doesn't work here. Give me that agate, or you'll never see your father!" As she charged him, he grabbed onto her.

With so much turmoil going on in the dungeon, Batty was able to get Gundar's troops inside the castle, and the dragon that fought with Vindamar soared high above everyone's heads. It wasn't until the dragon let out a roar that anyone noticed him.

Vindamar wasn't willing to give Paige up. He dragged her to the front altar where he had prepared to marry her. With no time to waste, he took the chalice filled with poison and put it to her lips even as she struggled, and then he started to chant. "Ellishm du noteum ell ventodemuse!"

The castle shook as if from an earthquake, and part of the floor cracked open. Dark smoke rose out of the pits below and formed gray clouds over Vindamar and Paige. Bugs came out of the cracked floor, and the foul stench of death filled the air. Tentacles filled with hissing faces of unimaginable monsters emerged from the open pit in the floor and crawled toward them.

"You shall drink, or I shall open the gates of the underworld!" Vindamar demanded.

Paige turned her head away from the chalice just as the dragon swooped down and sank his talons deep into Vindamar's back. Gundar and his troops made their way into the dungeon in time to watch the dragon violently shake Vindamar in the air. The dragon flew over the pit Vindamar had opened and dropped Vindamar into it.

At that moment, Gundar shouted to Paige and tossed her the staff. She caught it and held it high into the air, knowing exactly what to chant. "Eht s'rotaerc sesimorp llahs ed dellifluf. Rof eht ssensuoethgir seirc fo ssertsid sah neeb draeh. Og won otni eht tip fo erif. Rof uoy llahs eb delpmart toofrednu." She continued her chant until the creatures followed Vindamar back into the pit he had opened. And then the pit sealed once more.

The dragon flew several times around Paige before it collapsed inches from her feet. She fell to her knees and looked at the dragon. "You are the dragon who saved me not once but three times. Who are you?"

Then she noticed the dewdrop crystal embedded in its heart. "Noah!" she cried, and lifted the dragon's head gently to rest on her lap. "Oh, Noah, it is you." She wept as she cradled him. "You can't die—I need you. Please, Noah, open your eyes."

Paige leaned over to kiss the dragon, and when she did, a tear rolled down her cheek and dripped onto his forehead. The dragon slowly started to change his form. The scales started to look like human skin, and the wings became arms. Soon his transformation back to human was complete.

He opened his eyes and looked up at her. "Paige, we did it. Vindamar can't hurt either one of us anymore," he said softly. "I need you to go and bring Gundar to me."

Gundar spoke up. "I'm already here, Noah."

"Gundar, you fought well, dear friend. I have one more request for you."

"Try not to speak now, my King." Gundar bent down so Noah could see him.

"I don't have much time," he said, and coughed up blood. "I have the Piasa outside waiting to take you, Paige, and the crystal. Paige has to return the crystal back to where it belongs. She must go now if we want Vindamar's reign of terror to end."

Noah turned and looked into Paige's tearful eyes. "My sweet, beautiful Paige, you need to listen to me. I want you to take the crystal and return it back to its rightful place. It belongs in the meadow of Amaranth."

"No! If I pull the crystal out, you will die. I'll send for my grandmother—she'll make you better. She's a wizard, and she'll know what to do." She scrambled to find the agate. "Look, I have the agate. It gives the Zandorians power. Maybe it will help you, too." She placed it in his hand.

"No, Paige, listen! Everyone, including me, is counting on you. You need to leave and get the crystal back before it's too late for life to be restored to the Zandorian Kingdom."

Noah didn't say another word. He just gazed into Paige's eyes as he pulled the crystal out of his chest. His eyes closed, and then he went limp.

CHAPTER 33

RETURN OF THE DEWDROP CRYSTAL

Paige cradled Noah in her arms as she wept; she didn't want to let him go. It took most of Gundar's army to pry her away from him.

"Paige, we have to go," Gundar said as he wrapped the dewdrop crystal in linen. "I promise Noah will have a suitable burial, but we need to honor his request and get the crystal back as soon as possible."

"You're right." She stood up from where she once held Noah and wiped her tears away. "He sacrificed his life so this crystal could be returned...so it will be."

She reluctantly left Noah, and Gundar escorted her back to the room that held her belongings.

"I believe this belongs to you." he said as he handed Paige her coin.

She took the coin before she changed into her clothes. She went to place the coin into her pocket, but instead it fell onto the cold, cobblestone floor. She stared down at it, remembering what her grandmother told her, whoever holds this coin shall rule the world.

Paige grabbed the coin and left. Once outside, she stood on the bridge and yelled, "What good is this coin without you, Noah? I don't want it. Let the fate of the Zandorian gods determine its keeper," then tossed it into the murky waters below.

The only thing she took with her was her staff and the dewdrop crystal, leaving the agate with Noah and the coin lost in the water below.

Gundar helped Paige onto the Piasa, but Paige stopped him when he was about to climb up.

"No, Gundar. I can do this. Please stay and look after everything. I know you will make sure Noah is properly taken care of. The Piasa will take care of me and make sure I get where I'm supposed to go. I will complete my destiny."

"You have my word that I will take care of Noah personally," Gundar said.

"Now go and return the crystal."

And she did just that. She returned the crystal back to the meadow of Amaranth. With the crystal's return, strange things started to occur over the next few days. The rivers filled their dry beds with cool, sparkling water that housed every imaginable type of water creature. The sun brought warmth rather than scorching heat. Animals thought to be extinct reappeared, and young songbirds chirped in the trees. Even the songs of the dewdrops that had disappeared now danced in tune with the fireflies as the dew misted the land once more. Hope and prosperity returned for the people of Zandora, but Paige went on mourning for Noah. Losing him and failing to save her father tugged heavily at her heart.

Word had reached Gundar that Paige had not returned home to her grandmother, but had stayed in the canyon of Gaithe near Mela's grave. Gundar, being the friend and warrior he was, could not sit idle while Paige was still in so much pain, so he went to her.

"I was told I could find you here, and here you sit," Gundar said, approaching Paige at Mela's grave.

"Oh, Gundar," she cried, "I'm not sure if I should have come on this quest. So many have died, and for what?"

"Oh, I don't know," Gundar said as he sat next to Paige. "Look around you. What do you see? Maybe you should open your heart to what you have rather than mourn for what you've lost. You may be surprised what happens when you encounter and cherish what is rather than what was."

"I guess you're right, Gundar, but I don't know. Maybe—"

"I know I'm right. You won't know what's waiting for you if you don't seek out the answers you have in your heart. Trust me, Paige. It's time for you to go back to your randmother. It's where you belong."

"Will you come with me, Gundar?"

"I wouldn't miss this for the world." Gundar called out for the Piasa.

"Our princess is ready to go home. Take us to the river of Erainna, where Morwenna awaits."

The Piasa lowered his enormous wings so Paige and Gundar could get on his back, and then he delivered them to the river of Erainna where Paige had last seen her grandmother.

Neither spoke as they watched the river.

"What a beautiful moon we're having tonight," someone said from behind.

Paige turned toward the voice. "Grandma!" she cried as she ran into her grandmother's arms. "I've missed you so much."

"I've missed you too, Autumn Mist."

The two embraced for the longest time before Morwenna whispered into her ear.

"My sweet Autumn Mist, you have cried so many tears and have endured so much, but in return you have restored so much."

She wiped Paige's tears away. "Put your staff into the river."

As Paige placed her staff into the river, Morwenna chanted. "Eht efil taht ecno saw llahs emoc niaga."

Little stars fell from the night sky and covered the river. The seahorses that had been under Vindamar's spell emerged—including Paige's father.

"Father!" she squealed and ran into the river to hug him.

"Paige! My angel," he grabbed her and swung her around. "I thought I would never get to see or hold you or your mother again." Like the day she was born her father rejoiced as he held her in his arms.

Morwenna met the two as they came out of the water. "You have done it, Autumn Mist! You have brought balance back to our lives, and you've brought your father home."

Morwenna, Autumn Mist, Gundar, and her father laughed, told stories, and danced under the light of the moon alongside the fairies, Zandarians, and Andalarians who had come out of the river.

"Look, Autumn Mist," said Morwenna. "Do you recognize anyone coming toward us?"

Paige looked down the path she started on, now illuminated by the huge moon overhead. There was Atwood, Mela, and her pups. "You're alive!" Paige gasped as she ran toward them. "I can't believe it! Everyone is here. I thought I lost all of you forever."

She looked for Noah too, but she didn't see him. Her heart grew somber. "What about Noah? Grandma, can't he come back, too? Where is he?"

Morwenna smiled, as she waved her arms to open the porthole. "Well, dear, that's another journey."

And story.

www.ingramcontent.com/pod-product-compliance
Lightning Source LLC
Chambersburg PA
CBHW071945190726
48293CB00004B/1352